C000313053

How to teach
Primary Music

100
INSPIRING IDEAS

David Wheway, Hilary Miles
and Jonathan Barnes

This book is produced from independently certified FSC paper to ensure responsible forest management.

For more information visit: **www.harpercollins.co.uk/green**

William Collins' dream of knowledge for all began with the publication of his first book in 1819.

A self-educated mill worker, he not only enriched millions of lives, but also founded a flourishing publishing house. Today, staying true to this spirit, Collins books are packed with inspiration, innovation and practical expertise. They place you at the centre of a world of possibility and give you exactly what you need to explore it. Collins. Freedom to teach.

An imprint of HarperCollins*Publishers*
The News Building
1 London Bridge Street
London
SE1 9GF

www.collins.co.uk

© HarperCollins*Publishers* 2017

10 9 8 7 6 5 4 3 2 1

ISBN 978-1-4729-2738-5

British Library Cataloguing in Publication Data
A catalogue record for this publication is available from the British Library.

Authors: David Wheway, Hilary Miles, Jonathan Barnes
Commissioning editor: Mary Chandler
Development editor: Em Wilson
Project editor: Alexander Rutherford
Proofreader: Sue Chapple
Cover designer: Angela English
Internal designer: Ken Vail Graphic Design
Production controller: Sarah Burke
Printed and bound by Caligraving Ltd

Acknowledgements

The authors and publisher would like to thank the following for allowing the inclusion of their ideas in this resource: Cherry Tewfik for Idea 2 'Switch 1', Idea 6 'All about me'; Idea 10 'Choosing a song using a present box', Idea 24 'Conductor game'. Shelagh Thompson for agreeing to the inclusion of Idea 13 'Sound stories' and Idea 41 'Sound chance' adapted from ideas in Explore Music Across the Curriculum by Wheway, D. and Thompson, S. (2002). Loughborough: LMPi

Table of contents

Creative starting points

Active listening

Music in the environment

Introduction

Welcome!

You are clearly someone interested in developing music for the children you teach. Maybe you are about to embark on teaching music for the first time, and anxious about your knowledge and abilities. Or perhaps you are looking for further ideas, or materials to support you and your colleagues.

Since the introduction of the National Curriculum in the UK (as well as the 'National plan'), there has been (in spirit), a commitment to ensure that all children enjoy a broad and balanced curriculum that includes music. However, teachers can feel unsupported or de-skilled in music teaching, either through limited initial teacher education, or local and national priorities effectively pushing music aside.

'But – I'm not musical!'

This book has been written by people who have years of experience working with teachers who are very anxious (often 'terrified') about teaching music. The authors understand such anxieties and have developed ways of working that are engaging and fun – but which still have music learning at the heart of the activities.

Role models in teaching

In music, teachers are often dissuaded, rather than inspired, by someone with advanced instrumental or vocal skills. Teachers recognise such skills have been honed over many years, and cannot be quickly acquired. However, developing children's musical skills in the primary classroom can be more playful, and less reliant on the knowledge and skills of the teacher. It is as much about pedagogy as it is about skills.

100 ideas for music teaching

This book aims to promote activities that:

❍ are easy to teach whilst still promoting good music knowledge and skills

❍ are inclusive

❍ approach learning in playful ways whilst developing confidence in the children.

Such activities ensure music sits within the curriculum as a regular aspect of children's holistic learning experience.

How to use this book

Dip into this book whenever you want a flash of inspiration to improve and inspire your primary music teaching.

The ideas in this book are organised by theme – these are given at the foot of each page. Each idea follows a very simple format:

❍ **Title:** the catchy title sums up what the idea is about.

❍ **Quote:** the opening quote from a teacher or student captures the essence of the idea.

❍ **Overview:** the quick overview of the idea will help you select a new idea to read or re-find an idea you found useful on a previous flick-through.

❍ **Idea:** the idea itself.

❍ **Hints and tips:** additional tips, suggestions for ways to take the idea further and bonus ideas are provided throughout.

First lesson 1

"The children were great — it was me who got muddled!"

If you're looking for a simple but effective activity for your first lesson that's easy to deliver and gets children to engage actively with music, try this simple clapping game: it's all about maintaining a steady beat, which is fundamental to music-making.

Age: Basic activity 6–7 years; extension for older children

Basic activity

○ Send a clap all the way round the circle (you clap, next child claps, and so on).

○ Ask the children what they noticed, e.g. 'It got faster', 'Not everyone clapped at the right time', and so on.

○ Congratulate the children for their observations and, more importantly, good listening skills.

○ Repeat the activity going in the opposite direction. Simply ask the children to 'listen carefully' this time.

○ Was the response similar or was it improved?

Rebound

○ As the clap goes round the circle, anyone can say 'change' or 'ping' instead of clapping – making the clap go in the opposite direction.

○ Practise in small groups to ensure everyone in each circle gets to pass the beat.

Extension

○ As each child claps, they turn to the person next to them in the circle to indicate it's their turn to clap next. Instead of saying 'change' (or 'ping'), they send the clap in the opposite direction by turning back to the person who just clapped. This is fun – but very easy to get in a muddle. If this happens, simply stop – and re-start the activity from where it became muddled.

Top tip

Avoid beginning music lessons with rules or too much talk. Ensure children are immediately active. That way, you will convince children that this is a lesson they are going to enjoy.

Bonus idea

If the children manage the extension well, try incorporating clapping across the circle by pointing at an individual with the clapped hands as well as changing direction.

2 Switch 1

"This activity really develops the children's attention."

In this game, a child sets up a movement, rhythm or sound to recorded music for others to copy.

Age: 4–6 (particularly good for children with SEND)

Resources: Recorded music with a strong beat (e.g. pop music, march music); a selection of untuned percussion instruments (optional)

Taking it further...

Call 'Switch!' as you switch to a new movement. The children have to watch carefully to try to switch quickly.

Bonus idea !

Share out tapping, scraping and shaking instruments (one per child). On the word 'Switch' you mime tapping, shaking or scraping an instrument. Children with the corresponding instruments play the beat in response.

● Start the recorded music.

● Demonstrate a moving action in time to the beat (e.g. clapping, waving, hand jive, tapping shoulders, etc.).

● Ask the children to copy your action.

● Now call out the name of a child to start a new action to the continuing recorded music.

● This child takes over, everyone now copying their action. When they are ready they say the name for a new leader (another child).

● This continues until everyone who wants has had a turn, or the time (or music) runs out.

Get with the beat

"It's challenging trying to fit in longer names."

Children love the personal recognition this game provides. It focuses on developing and maintaining a steady beat – but has the additional challenge of fitting the syllables of one's name to the beat.

Age: 7+

Setting the pattern

○ Standing in a circle, count 1, 2, 3, 4, 1, 2, 3, 4 repeatedly to a steady, slow beat.

○ Encourage the children to join in accurately. If this is tricky, try walking on the spot: left, 2, 3, 4, left, 2, 3, 4…

○ When this is secure, ask the children to alternate four beats clapping with four beats silent clapping: everyone claps and says '1, 2, 3, 4', then claps the air for four beats with the back of their hands, saying 'rest, 2, 3, 4'.

○ Try not speaking with the four silent beats. Can the children come back in for the next count of 4?

Name rhythms

○ Once the pattern is established, go round the circle for each child in turn to say their name rhythmically in the four quiet beats. This might just be their first name, or first and second name, depending on the age/ability of the children, e.g.

Top tip

A 'rest' in music is a silent beat – so tap the air as quietly as possible. If you are anxious about maintaining a steady beat, try using an online metronome or an app to accompany the activity, adjusting the tempo to a comfortable speed.

Taking it further...

If children are confident, try changing to clapping then resting for six beats, still ensuring a steady beat.

Bonus idea

Instead of saying their name, introduce a theme, such as favourite cars/food/ games/places.

1	2	3	4	rest	rest	rest	rest
Clap	Clap	Clap	Clap	San -	jay	rest	rest

Or:

1	2	3	4	rest	rest	rest	rest
Clap	Clap	Clap	Clap	He -	len	Wor-thing	-ton

4 Let sleeping dogs lie

"I didn't realise music could be such a quiet lesson!"

This activity encourages children to value quiet sounds and handle instruments with care.

Age: A good activity for all ages – depending on the type of instrument used.

Resources: Two or three percussion instruments (choose instruments that are easy or tricky to move without them making a sound, as appropriate to the age/experience of your children)

Music lessons, especially with percussion, can be exciting and potentially noisy, so this activity can introduce a period of calm, with children working together to gain quietness. It is a popular activity and many teachers use it at other points in the day. It also promotes the notion of quietness in music – which composers use for effect.

Top tip

It is not unusual to have at least one child who might want to make a sound on purpose. One solution is to have them last in the circle, to disrupt the activity less and so the rest of the group feel they have achieved the objective.

Taking it further...

Try passing two or even three instruments around the circle. Make it even trickier, by passing instruments in opposite directions.

The objective is to pass an instrument around the circle without waking the 'sleeping dog' (puppet, child with eyes closed).

● Choose one child to be the 'sleeping dog' in the centre of the circle (or use a puppet). Having a child with eyes closed as the 'sleeping dog' can make the activity feel more challenging.

● Start with an instrument that is easier to control, such as a woodblock.

● You pass the instrument to the next person in the circle without it making a sound. That child then passes it silently to the next person, and so on.

● Ensure each child who passes well gets a thumbs up (or similar) from you.

● The sleeping dog raises a hand each time they hear a sound.

● Explore passing gradually less easy percussion instruments (bells are very hard) as children exert more control.

Balloon ride 5

"This activity shows that we can all have a broad pitch range."

By following an imaginary hot-air balloon, children learn to control the pitch of their voices and develop an awareness of the varied pitch of their voices – important for vocal development and singing. This is a good activity to do whenever there are a few minutes to spare during the day.

Age: 6–8

Resources: A cut-out hot-air balloon on a stick

Take the children on an imaginary hot-air balloon ride. Move the balloon higher and lower for children to match with their voices.

● As the balloon slowly rises the children hum higher and higher (taking breaths when needed), and as it slowly loses altitude they hum lower and lower. (Children will generally tend to find a common pitch without instruction, or leading. If this isn't the case, you can help by humming with them).

● The balloon can rise and fall a number of times. Can the children make their pitched humming higher and lower as appropriate?

● Ask a child to control the hot-air balloon. Listen out to the children's humming to ensure they aren't taken uncomfortably high or low.

● Later on, try different sustained vocal sounds, e.g. 'oo', 'ahh', 'nnn'. These are good for vocal development.

Top tip

Encourage the children to let their sound out slowly so that they can keep the sound going for longer before they need to take a breath.

Taking it further...

When taking in a breath, encourage children to take it from down in their tummies rather than their chests.
● Try singing a well-known tune using some of the vocal sounds given here, rather than the words.

6 All about me

"Can we sing a song about me and my friends?"

This idea offers a simple and enjoyable way to compose songs about the people and everyday activities in class.

Age: Early Years (particularly useful for children with SEND)

Resources: A guitar if anyone can play it, otherwise voices are fine

Top tip

Practise at home first with personalised songs about friends. For inspiration, look at the 'The Lullaby Project' videos on the Groundswell Arts website (**groundswellarts. com**).

Taking it further...

Make up songs for different times of the school day, e.g. tidy-up time, lunchtime, home time, etc.

Bonus idea

Some children may be able to make up their own songs in pairs or groups.

Think of a well-known song and substitute the words with new ones to suit any occasion. For example:

❍ To the tune of *Drunken sailor*, exchange words with the name of someone in the class, e.g. 'What shall we do with Annie Slater?'.

❍ To the tune of *Twinkle, Twinkle* – make up fun lyrics using the names of children in the class. Children could help with the words, e.g.

Stephen has got bright green toes,

Craig has got a purple nose,

Ibra's smiling all day long,

Bella's singing a lovely song, etc.

❍ To *The wheels on the bus*:

Keziah's coming into class, into class, into class ... all day long.

David's got a sniffy nose, sniffy nose, sniffy nose ... all day long.

Children love hearing songs about themselves, their shoes, their favourite toy, a pet dog, an aunt/uncle in another country, and so on.

Two-note songs **7**

"You can sing about anything using this idea."

In this idea, only two notes are used to make up songs, and the subject can be anything you wish. By using a very simple melody and making the song personal, your children's singing confidence will be enhanced.

Age: 3–5

For this activity, you simply sing the same interval as a ding-dong doorbell, or when you call, 'cooeee!' (these are also the first two notes of *Swing low, sweet chariot*). You use this interval to sing questions for the children to respond back in song.

○ All sit in a circle. Sing a question to all the children, such as:

upper note: x   x

lower note: x   x

          Who   likes   ice - cream?

○ Any children who like ice cream sing back:

x   x

   x   x

I   like   ice - cream?

○ Try other questions about games, pets, birthdays, breakfast, etc.

○ By carefully selecting questions, you can get just a few children singing or even just one child. For example, if a child tells you first thing in the morning that they have a new baby sister:

x   x   x

      x   x   x   x   x

Who's   just   got   a   ba - by   sis - ter?

x   x   x

      x   x   x   x   x

I've   just   got   a   ba - by   sis - ter?

> **Top tip**
>
> Try to find a pitch that is comfortable for your children, rather than expecting them to match your comfortable pitch.

> **Taking it further...**
>
> Sing these simple two-note songs at any point during the day to question, comment, and create a relaxed atmosphere, e.g. 'Who's sitting ready to begin?' 'Well done Chloe you've worked really well.' 'Thank you Rajesh for tidying the shelves.' 'Ge-orge, don't do that.' 'Who knows where the hamster's gone?'

8 Listen and move

"This idea really develops their listening!"

Develop children's attention and listening skills with this simple movement activity.

Age: 6+

Resources: 2–4 items of percussion, initially with distinctly different sounds (e.g. claves, tambourine, drum, bells); another adult if possible

Taking it further...

Use sounds that are much more difficult to distinguish from each other (e.g. claves and different types of woodblock). You could also introduce two different sounds for turning 90 degrees to the left and 90 degrees to the right.

Bonus idea

Utilise the playground or other outdoor area and adapt the game, e.g.
○ Use a compass to establish north then direct children to turn north, south, east and west by sound.
○ Children, in groups, then guide a child round an obstacle course (e.g. a route of beanbags or round other children – see Idea 59).

○ Children stand in a large space, all facing in one direction.

○ Play one of the instruments very briefly. Tell them that, whenever they hear that sound, they should take a step forward. Try playing a few times to check they understand.

○ Introduce a second instrument sound – for a step backwards.

○ The children step forwards or backwards according to the sequence of sounds you play.

○ If children cope well with this, you can introduce other movements to other sounds, such as a step to the left, a step to the right. You will probably welcome at least one other person helping with playing the instruments – which could be another adult, or some confident children.

Animal ostinati 9

"This was just hilarious!"

An ostinato is a repeated pattern. Creating ostinato patterns with vocal sounds is both fun and challenging. In this example farmyard sounds have been suggested, but other themes might be introduced – possibly linked to a class focus.

Age: 5–7 (see 'Taking it further' for adapting this activity with children aged 8–11)

No instruments are required for this activity – the resulting piece is purely vocal.

● Ask the children to think of single syllable sounds they might hear on a farm (e.g. quack, moo, oink, woof, baa, cluck…). Perhaps the farmer could join in with the sheepdog's name, e.g. 'Jess!'

● Now introduce a steady and repeated count of four – ask children to join in the count.

● Once a nice steady count has been established, ask all the children to choose a number between one and four, and choose a sound – they will perform their chosen sound on the chosen count.

● Check that at least three numbers have someone making a sound, then repeat the count – but this time children are silent except on their chosen beat.

● Count 1, 2, 3, 4 repeatedly with the children making their sound each time on their number.

Consider performing the finished piece to parents at the end of the school day.

Top tip

If possible, mark the beat visually as well as saying the count, e.g. move one hand down (HD) on every count of one: HD – 2 – 3 – 4 – HD – 2 – 3 – 4 …

Taking it further...

For older children and those who can easily manage the four-beat ostinato, encourage them to select two numbers between one and eight on which they will make their sound. For even greater challenge, try repeating patterns of five or seven.

Bonus idea

Divide the class in two. One half sets up a repeating pattern of four or eight with their farmyard sounds. Once it is established, the other half sings *Old MacDonald* at the same time in time to the beat. Another adult would be helpful here to support this group.

10 Choosing a song using a present box

"I need help to choose which song to sing."

In this activity, children find object symbols to represent a bank of well-known songs and then play a simple game to choose 'their' song. The activity becomes progressively more symbolic. The activity encourages turn-taking, sharing, singing together and ownership of a song.

Age: 4–6 (particularly useful for children with SEND)

Resources: Plastic-lidded see-through box; different coloured tissue paper; objects related to song titles; plain paper, card and coloured pens; Makaton symbol bank; music that can be stopped/started

In advance of playing the game, collect objects from around the classroom with the children that could symbolise different well-known songs, e.g. a bus (*The wheels on the bus*), a star (*Twinkle twinkle*), some soft animals (*Old MacDonald*), etc. Then wrap each object in a different coloured piece of tissue paper and put them in a box to look like presents.

Taking it further...

For songs with multiple verses (e.g. *Old MacDonald*, *The wheels on the bus*), create pictures/symbols for each verse that can later be physically arranged to remind children of the sequence of the song (e.g. include wipers, horn, door, etc.).

Bonus idea !

Consider turning some of the songs into graphic notation.

Basic game

O Pass the box round the circle like a 'pass the parcel' game. Ask one child to start and stop the music without looking at who is going to open the parcel.

O When the music stops, the child with the box chooses a 'present', unwraps it, and guesses the song it represents. Others can help if necessary.

O The class sings the song together and the game continues.

Developing the game

Instead of wrapped 'presents' you or the children create packs of picture cards (pictorial representations of the presents, or graphic symbols of the sounds). See Idea 48 - Graphic Scores.

Stone passing song **11**

"We play and sing this in the playground too."

Stone passing songs are used throughout Africa. They teach pulse and rhythm in a fun way and rely on everyone playing and singing their part.

Age: 6–11

Resources: Stones (small enough to pass easily) or plastic cups – one per child

This activity works with any song with a strong pulse. For a more authentic approach, explore African songs such as *Obwisana san* (see 'Top tip').

❍ Sitting in a circle, distribute one stone per child.

❍ Children get to know their stone, give it a name or mark it in some way.

❍ Each child places their stone in front of them.

❍ Set a steady beat and ask the children to use their right hand (or left if they prefer) to lift the stone up on beat one and then place it on the floor in front of their neighbour to their right on beat two.

❍ Introduce a song and practise singing and passing, first without letting go of the stones but emphasising how everyone will pick up and place at the same time.

❍ Once confident singing and moving, each child lets go of 'their' stone so that it (and everyone else's) gets passed around during the song. The song ends when everyone gets their stone back.

Top tip

There is a video clip of this activity being performed using the song *Obwisana san* on the *How to teach Primary Music* page at **dwheway.wikispaces. com/100+ideas+ Music** Children enjoy having their own stone, but if you haven't got enough stones you could always use alternatives, such as unifix cubes, though they are not quite so personal.

Taking it further...

Try different patterns of stone movement, e.g. pick up, show stone to circle, bring back to self, pass on. You could ask children to invent their own passing patterns.

Bonus idea ❗

Make this into a performance with drummers and instrumentalists.

1	2	1	2	1	2	1	2
(pick up)		(put down)		(pick up)		(put down)	
Ob-wi-	*sa-na*	*sa -*	*na*	*ob-wi-*	*sa-na*	*san*	

12 Puppet play

"Although we use puppets a lot, I hadn't thought of using them in music. This worked really well."

This activity is all about developing the ability to start and stop in response to signals. It works well at the start of a music lesson as it develops control and respect for the instruments, but also allows children to exhaust their natural physical inclination to just make lots of sound.

Age: 4–6

Resources: One percussion item per child; a puppet/soft toy

◐ Place an item of percussion in front of each child in the circle.

◐ Tell the children that once the activity begins they can play loudly and quietly, but not so loudly that they hurt the instrument.

Top tip

Organise your classroom by creating or finding enough space (e.g. by moving desks) for children to sit comfortably in a circle.

◐ Have the puppet or soft toy sit on your arm or knee. The puppet will 'dance' for a short while then pause – the children play when the puppet dances, and hold instruments still when the puppet pauses.

◐ Once the children are confident making and pausing sounds, use the puppet to encourage more sensitive playing, e.g. large/small movements to encourage loud/quieter playing, shivering for very quiet sounds, large to small/small to large movements for getting louder/quieter. (You'll find further ideas for adapting the puppet dance in Idea 40.)

Taking it further...

Children could work in smaller groups, with one puppet/soft toy per group.

◐ Encourage the children to take turns leading with the puppet. Support them by dancing with them if necessary.

Sound stories **13**

"So much better than asking children to respond to a story."

In this idea children explore percussion, and the teacher exploits children's sound suggestions to improvise a musical story. Children's attention is developed and their sounds valued.

Age: 4–6

Resources: small sets of similar percussion, with enough for one per child

Allocate a percussion instrument to each child.

❍ Devise clear start/stop signals for children to watch out for (e.g. raise hand for 'stop'). Develop subtle signals (e.g. touch the tip of your nose for 'stop' and the tip of your ear for 'start').

❍ Ask children to spend approximately 30 seconds exploring sounds they can make with their percussion instrument.

❍ Ask the children to think about what the sounds they discover remind them of (e.g. a child with a scraping instrument might say, 'a frog').

❍ Invite children to share their ideas. For each idea, ask if anyone else has a similar sound, e.g. for 'frog' there may be other children with scrapers, or different instruments who can also make a sound like a frog.

❍ Write down five suggestions on the interactive whiteboard or flipchart paper. They may be very random, e.g. 'frog', 'rain', 'Christmas', 'thunder', 'pebbles'.

❍ Make up a story using the words. When each word is used, pause to allow children to respond to the word by making their sounds – use the 'stop' signal, as appropriate. Don't worry if the story doesn't make much sense, the children will simply enjoy responding to the cues, e.g.

It was a rainy [sounds] Christmas day [sounds] and frog [sounds] was hopping along a pebbly beach [sounds]. Frog [sounds] could hear thunder [sounds] as he hopped along the pebbles [sounds], so expected the rain [sounds] to get faster because of the thunder [sounds]. Frog [sounds] had hoped for snow not thunder [sounds] and rain [sounds], at his home amongst the pebbles [sounds], for Christmas [sounds] to frog [sounds] was not Christmas [sounds] without snow, rather than thunder [sounds] and rain [sounds] on the pebbles [sounds]…

Taking it further...

Place a selection of instruments in the music area for children to explore sound associations further.

14 Percussion without the palaver

"I love these simple ideas that help me to control percussion lessons."

This guide to using percussion instruments in the classroom is particularly helpful when using percussion for the first time, and tackles one of the first challenges: handing out the instruments!

Age: All

If percussion isn't to be used immediately (perhaps there is a warm-up or other activity to start your session) keep the instruments to one side until needed. Let the children know when in the lesson you intend to use them, so they can concentrate on other things until the allotted time.

'Have a go' game

Play a game to let children have a go on the percussion instruments in a controlled but fun way before using them in an activity – for example, see Idea 12, where children start and stop playing to a puppet.

'Make the sound of' game

Ask children to play their instruments but ask for them to play like a lion roaring, a dream, a whisper, a tortoise, a butterfly, etc.

Percussion sets

To avoid children snatching at, or arguing over instruments, have percussion sets, which groups select in turn. Put the sets in something like coloured hoops, rather than children collecting from a music trolley where instruments can get tangled/jammed. Depending on time and aims, allow groups to explore sounds in different sets.

> **Top tip**
>
> Ensuring that you allow time for handing out and collecting in instruments encourages children to be responsible for and care for the instruments, and saves time in the long run.

Beaters last and first

Check whether an instrument needs beaters. Many drums are 'hand' drums (djembes, bongos, tambours…) so don't require a beater, whilst scraping instruments can utilise beater handles. Keep all beaters in a plastic bucket or crate, and go round the circle allowing children to select their beaters. At the end of a session, collect all beaters in, before the children return their instruments.

Percussion discussion

"I'm not confident teaching music because I don't know the names of all the instruments."

Below we give a brief introduction to some school percussion instruments. Remember, it is more important to know what type of instrument it is and how to play it, than know its name.

'Percussion' means that you strike or hit the instrument. Instruments can be divided into two main groups: 'tuned' and 'untuned':

❍ **Tuned percussion** (sometimes called 'pitched percussion') has tuned bars and can be used to play melodies. They include chime bars, xylophones (wooden bars), metallophones and glockenspiels (metal bars). Beaters are required (and different beaters will offer different qualities of sound – or *timbres*).

❍ **Untuned percussion** (sometimes called 'unpitched percussion') are shaken, scraped or tapped. They cannot be used to play melodies (even though they may have higher or lower pitches). It is fine to call an instrument a shaker, scraper or tapper, rather than by its name.

Schools should accumulate a range of percussion rather than lots of the same. Variety offers more performance and creative opportunities. Many music suppliers will have sets to purchase, and are normally very happy to discuss your requirements.

Beaters

Amass plenty of beaters, ideally two per child. Soft beaters are kinder on the ears, but small glockenspiels require smaller harder beaters. (Small all-in-one beaters are more child-proof).

Good technique should be encouraged, using a beater in each hand. Beaters are held between thumb and first finger with the hand on top. Keep wrist flexible and allow beaters to bounce. Avoid pointy fingers as this damps the sound. Play in the middle of the bar.

Top tip

Keep percussion well repaired (see Ideas 98–99). Poor or broken instruments should be replaced. Broken instruments can pose a health and safety risk.

Taking it further...

If you want to know the names of the different percussion instruments, try looking at online musical percussion catalogues (many music suppliers have these), or contact a supplier for a catalogue. At the time of writing, a good online resource is **lmsmusicsupplies. co.uk**.

16 Top tips for teaching music

"I liked the way you created space for the children. It made such a difference to how they interacted."

This idea gives a few of our top tips for teaching classroom music.

Classroom organisation

As a rule, make or find lots of space. Putting children in a large circle is especially good for passing games, working in pairs or small groups. There are social benefits that experienced teachers are quick to note, such as children building on observations of others, sharing ideas, having a clear view of the teacher/leader, feeling everyone is equal, not becoming anxious about 'mistakes', and so on.

Noise is good

The 'mess' in music is noise. Encouraging exploration and pupil talk means there will often be noise. Expect it. Read tips for specific activities to find ways to manage the noise (see also Idea 92).

Make music a regular feature

Children's music abilities will improve with regular opportunity, as will their attitudes. Avoid the pressure to prioritise other subjects over music.

Be prepared to have a go

Children will respect you for it. Let them know if you occasionally struggle (for instance in a rhythm game). Let children take the lead often. Above all, focus on the engagement, enjoyment and achievements of the children. Offer constructive praise, and seek advice on possible next steps.

Make time to plan your percussion resources

Consider when you might use percussion, what you will need and when the instruments will be collected. An inordinate amount of time can be spent setting up percussion if they are not stored appropriately (see also Ideas 15 and 98–99).

Top tip

Further advice can be found in the section 'Beyond the classroom' (Ideas 92–100).

Do it your way

All the activities in this book should be viewed as guidelines only. Bringing your own approach and owning the activity will ensure it becomes a class favourite.

Let's go disco-dancing 17

"Children worked really well, helping each other and inspiring others with their actions."

Children really appreciate activities that demand co-ordination. In this activity, simple movements are made more challenging by trying to maintain a steady beat whilst alternating movements with a partner.

Age: 7–11

Work with a child to model the activity to the rest of the class (and be prepared for children to laugh).

○ You and the child alternate saying 'one' and 'two': (You say 'One', the child says 'Two', you 'One', child 'Two'…). Repeat to a steady beat.

○ Create an action on your count (e.g. clap, raise an arm, touch your head, a dance move, a step…) and invite the child to invent their own movement.

○ Repeat the actions on each of your numbers.

Allow the children about 30 seconds to work in pairs to create their own alternating movements to a count of two.

Then, perform a whole class disco:

○ Organise the children in a circle in their pairs, so that all number 'ones' are standing to the left of their partners.

○ Set up a steady 1–2 beat and ask all children to perform their actions to the beat.

○ It should be relatively easy to observe if children are maintaining their action to the first or second beat, as actions alternate.

Repeat the activity, but this time ask the children, still working in pairs, to create a sequence of four actions to a repeated count of four beats.

Top tip

This is a very social activity. Notice how children may look across the circle to see what other children are doing, and how children support their partners. Note also how children might struggle but laugh about it – and still strive to improve.

Taking it further...

With children still in pairs, try a sequence to a count of three (both children initially sharing the three actions). Once the count of three begins, the children must try to alternate the three actions. This is much more difficult. A sequence of five would be even more challenging.

18 Desk drum kit

"I use this activity when a lesson finishes early. It's fun, and challenging."

A desk drum kit develops co-ordination through simple but challenging movements.

Age: 8–11

In this activity, children tap their hands on the desktop or their knees and their feet to create different drum patterns, following the key below:

LH = left hand   RH = right hand   LF = left foot   RF = right foot

lh lh = two taps with the left hand in the space of one count

❍ Children alternate left hand then right hand in time with a steady beat (perhaps say, 'left-right-left-right'…, to support).

❍ Once the beat is secure, repeat any/all of the following patterns:

Taking it further...

Could someone (adult, music hub, receiving secondary school) provide a drum kit and teach children some basic drumbeats?

Bonus idea !

Use iPads to challenge children further, such as with the drum kit in **GarageBand**.

1	2	3	4	
LH	RH	lh lh	RH	(repeat)

1	2	3	4	
LH	RH	LF	RF	(repeat)

1	2	3	4	
LH	rh rh	LF	LF	(repeat)

1	2	3	4	
lh lh	RF	RH	LF	(repeat)

❍ In groups, children combine any of the above.

● Individually, combine two rows simultaneously, e.g. (patterns)

1	2	3	4	
RH	rh rh	rh rh	RH	(repeat)
LH		LH		

Or

1	2	3	4	
rh rh	rh rh	rh rh	rh rh	(repeat)
LH	RF	LH	RF	

● Children create their own patterns.

Try some of the following patterns or ask children to create their own using the template below.

Further suggestions

1	2	3	4
lh lh	rh rh	rh rh	rh rh
RF	LF	LF	LF

1	2	3	4
LH	rh rh	LH	rh rh
rf rf	LF	rf rf	LF

Providing a template for the children (as illustrated) means they get creative quickly instead of spending time drawing their own templates.

TEMPLATE

1	2	3	4

19 Switch 2

"I try to think ahead what actions I will do."

This activity develops 'Switch 1' (see Idea 2), offering challenge through beat-keeping, co-ordination and recall skills.

Age: 6–11

Resources: Recorded music with a strong beat (optional)

Recorded music with a strong beat can support this activity.

○ Set up a steady clapped beat and ask children to join in.

○ Once everyone is clapping well, change the action from clapping to tapping shoulders. Children keep clapping and change only when you say 'Switch'.

○ Once this new action is established, change to a new action, (tapping head, touching alternate elbows, etc.). Children wait until you say 'Switch' before joining you. Continue changing actions in this way.

○ Try adding combinations of actions to the sequence (e.g. Shoulders – Head – Shoulders – Head, as one action)

○ Choose a child to lead.

Extending the idea further

Delay saying 'Switch' until you have moved on two sequences, e.g.

○ Start by clapping, then change to tapping head (children continue clapping as you haven't said 'Switch').

Bonus idea

One child hides whilst another is chosen as leader. The lead child sets up an action – changing occasionally but without saying 'Switch'. The hiding child returns and whilst the sequence continues has to identify the leader.

○ Change your action again to touching alternate elbows (children are still clapping; they can't change as you haven't said 'Switch').

○ NOW you say 'Switch'.

○ Children change to your second action (tapping your head). Meanwhile, you continue touching alternate elbows and perhaps choose a new action.

"The use of the rhythm grids was very inclusive."

These grids promote the ability to maintain a steady beat, whilst recording with very simple notation. Children of any age and ability can participate.

Age: Early Years – age 7+

Resources: Rhythm grids displayed on a flip chart or interactive whiteboard

Early Years/beginners

○ Display a rhythm grid (see right):

○ Tap each cell in the grid from left to right and moving down the grid from top to bottom row.

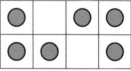

○ Invite children to clap each cell as you move through the grid again.

○ Ask a child to delete (cross out/move/wipe clean) the bubble in one of the cells.

○ Move through the grid again – but this time the children acknowledge the empty cell with a silent beat (rest). They might do this by tapping the air with the back of their hands.

○ Ask another child to delete a second bubble and perform that pattern together.

○ Provide blank grids for children to create their own rhythm grids with rests.

○ When they can play with an accurate beat, let them interpret the grids on percussion.

Age 5–8

The activity works as above, but the rhythm grids now have two different symbols so the class can be divided into two large groups (one group to play each symbol), and the grids can become more complex (e.g. 4 × 4, 5 × 4, 7 × 3).

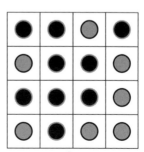

Once the children are confident clapping the more complex grids in two groups, they can develop the ideas further, e.g.

○ Invite children to consider different ways of interpreting the notations, such as loud/quiet, high/low voices, metal/wooden soundmakers, etc.

○ Encourage the children to be inventive in deciding ways to interpret the grids (e.g. using movement or funny sounds, etc.).

○ Provide blank grids for children to create their own patterns, interpreting the notations on a variety of sound sources/instruments.

Age 8+

Now include notations representative of words with two or more syllables, e.g. 'spi-der', in which each syllable is equal to half a beat. The example grid on the right shows ants and spiders.

Line one in this example would be said/clapped/played:

1	2	3 +	4
Ant	Ant	Spi - der	Ant
Clap	Clap	clap clap	Clap

○ As before, children work in groups to create their own grids, and explore different sound sources (voices, percussion, junk percussion, etc.).

Children can add three- and/or four-syllable words – but they will need to ensure the tempo (speed) is slow enough for the three- or four-syllable words to be said/clapped/played.

Crazy grids

"The children came up with really inventive ideas."

Children can be really inventive with rhythm grids. In this version, they explore their immediate environment, or their homes (with permission!), their voices and the potential for sounds from their bodies – with reservations!

Age: 7+

This idea builds on the rhythm grids introduced in Idea 20.

Tell the children they are going to create a rhythm grid, but that they have to find the most unusual, perhaps even outrageous or hilarious sounds they can. They might do this within a lesson, or be set the task a week ahead, to allow time for them to explore their environments and come up with unusual sounds.

It is a good idea to have some ideas yourself, to help children who struggle. Here are some ideas to get you started:

◉ Classroom: tap paint pots, rattle pencil cups, shut a large book with a bang, scrape a radiator, blow a raspberry on a tambour skin, flap paper on a flip chart, swirl beads in a round tin, etc.

◉ Home: bring in kitchen pots and pans, use a cooling tray like a washboard, create a shaker out of a plastic screw-top bottle, make claves out of wooden spoons, a wobble board (if parent will make one!), make a hose-pipe trumpet, blow a fizzy drinks bottle as a 'flute', etc.

◉ Outdoors: dried leaves, objects for shakers (such as shells, acorns/seeds, small stones), grass trumpet, etc.

◉ Vocal: shouts, hums, whistles, owl hoots, animal sounds, etc.

Top tip

Search online for some additional ideas. Some ideas are included for you on the *100 ideas Music* page at **dwheway.wikispaces. com/100+ideas +Music** – see 'Junk percussion ideas 1–3'.

Bonus idea

Explore sounds using apps such as: **MadPad HD** and/or **Music Mike Create** (see Ideas 79–80).

22 Singing tennis

"This game is fantastic — the children are singing, and learning about syllables."

This idea is very easy to plan for, but challenging to do. It helps children learn about beat, rhythm and lyrics, as well as sentence structure.

Age: 8+

For this activity, choose a short, simple song to start with (e.g. *A sailor went to sea* or *Frère Jacques*):

● Divide the class into two large groups who stand in two long lines facing each other. You stand between the groups.

Top tip

Sing the songs very slowly at first, and increase the tempo (speed) as children gain in confidence and ability.

● Explain that you are going to divide the song up into syllables, and that the two groups will take turns to sing each syllable in sequence, like a game of tennis, e.g.

Group 1	Group 2
A sai -	
lor	went
to sea,	
sea,	sea…

● This song is relatively easy, as each syllable is sung on the beat.

● Try a more challenging song (e.g. *God save the queen*) in which the rhythm has to be maintained as each syllable is sung in turn, e.g.

Taking it further...

Children could practise and present in smaller groups their own 'tennis' songs.

Group 1	Group 2
God	save
our	gra -
cious	queen…

You will notice, the syllable 'gra-' takes the time of two beats. The teacher (or leader) will need to wait for two beats before pointing to the opposite group, to keep the rhythm of the song.

● Invite a confident child to be the conductor.

Bonus idea

As you and your class become more confident with this activity, explore some songs from around the world, e.g. *Funga Alafia* (available online).

Create a simple melody **23**

"It's good to see how the children can think for themselves."

In this idea, children learn that melodies move by small or large jumps, or steps. They explore and create their own melodies.

Age: 6+

Resources: Tuned percussion (xylophones, metallophones, glockenspiels or chime bar sets, see Idea 15)

Before introducing the instruments, sing a few familiar songs and demonstrate that the melodies move by steps and jumps.

● Sing the opening of *Hot cross buns:* notice how it starts quite high ('Hot'), takes a very big jump down in pitch ('cross'), and then takes a medium-sized jump upwards ('buns'). On a xylophone try playing, high C – low C, then middle G to play the first three notes of this tune.

● Sing the opening of *Three blind mice:* notice how it takes three steps downwards, repeats, then repeats the same pattern at a higher pitch (try playing E – D – C, E – D – C, G – F – F – E, G – F – F – E).

Show the children the pattern of notes for a 'pentatonic' (five-note) scale: C D E F G.

Distribute as many sets of tuned percussion as possible. Children might work in pairs at a xylophone. Explore the notes together:

● Allow a few seconds for the children to explore the pattern of notes C D E F G.

● Ask the children to demonstrate playing small jumps using the given notes (e.g. C–E, A–E, D–A, etc.)

Top tip

The xylophones you are using may have different bars – or even some missing. Make the best of the notes you have – but do re-order missing bars. Likewise, keep the xylophones in a good state of repair. If you are unsure of maintenance, email a photo of the percussion piece to the shop from which you are ordering.

To create a simple melody:

● Ask each child (in turn if sharing) to use steps and jumps to invent a short melody to the words, 'Simple Simon met a pie-man'. Each child has about one minute to find a melody they can remember, and repeat over and over.

● Count in, 1 2 3 4, and everyone plays their melodies together – reciting the words.

● Each child now has their own melody (which they can call melody 'A'). Encourage them to go on to invent a different melody (which they can call 'B') to the words 'Go-ing to the fair' (which will have a silent beat at the end).

● Once everyone has two melodies, explore a simple sequence for the two melodies (e.g. Melody 'A' followed by 'B' followed by 'B' finishing with 'A').

● All play their melodic sequence together after your count in.

Extending the idea for older children

Set up tuned percussion in a music area (see Idea 31), with any of the arrangements of notes below for children to explore creating short melodies. The different arrangements of notes will each produce a different feel:

● C D E F G A B

● A B C D E F G

● Other pentatonic scales (e.g. F G A C D, or all sharps ♯ and flats ♭)

● C D E F♯ G♯ B♭ (Tuned percussion often comes with spare B♭'s and F♯'s. G♯ bars can be ordered from suppliers.)

● E F♯ G B♭ B

Taking it further...

Encourage children to explore longer sequences.

Conductor game **24**

"Everybody gets a turn in this one."

Children take control of starting and stopping and changing dynamics. The activity encourages eye contact, attention, turn-taking, and controlling sounds together as a group.

Age: 5–7 (particularly good for children with SEND)

Resources: Three sets of dynamics cards (loud and quiet); song cards (giving the names of some well-known songs); sets of tuned and untuned percussion instruments (e.g. chime bars notes C and G, drums and tappers, bells and scrapers)

○ Sing a well-known song together.

○ Children respond when you call 'start' and 'stop', e.g.
Oh, the grand old Duke of York
He had ten thousand men. (Teacher: 'Stop!')
(Teacher: 'Start!') *He marched them up to the top of the hill,*
And he marched them down again. ('Stop')
Repeat – stopping in different places.

○ In this example, the song is paused at the end of a line (phrase). Stopping in the middle of a phrase can be more challenging.

○ Use only hand signs: hold hands together for silence, open them clearly for start. Alternatively, hold a hand up like a policeman stopping traffic for stop, wave on for go.

○ Children take turns conducting with help, then independently.

○ Introduce dynamics: demonstrate hands very slowly opening wide and closing again (without completely closing) indicating louder and quieter.

Develop the activity using three sets of song and dynamics cards:

○ Invite children one at a time to be the conductor.

○ Each conductor chooses a song card and arranges the dynamic cards into a sequence.

○ They lead the class in singing the song, holding up the dynamics cards in sequence.

Taking it further...

Allocate sets of instruments to three groups. Invite a volunteer to conduct each group. They play only when directed by their conductor – sometimes together, sometimes separately.

Bonus idea

Everyone sits in a circle with an instrument. The conductor stands in the middle and points to individuals or groups, who only play when directed. They keep playing as long as the conductor allows.

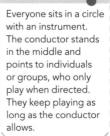

25 Rhythms for attention

"This is a great way to generate new rhythms for gaining children's attention."

Teachers often use clapped rhythms to gain attention in class time. Changing the rhythm regularly not only ensures more careful listening and attentiveness – it is also more fun. Using song lyrics is a great way to generate new rhythms.

Age: All (to suit complexity of the rhythm)

Simple clapped rhythms used to gain attention are sometimes limited in scope, and this brief moment can be used to develop children's musicality. Having a range of phrases in one's head (or written down) can make the attention gain more interesting and musically challenging. These rhythms can be spoken (as long as the lyrics are 'safe') whilst clapping, or just clapped. Spend a few more seconds to clap the chosen rhythm a few times to develop an accurate response.

Here are some sample rhythms to be clapped – use the first lines from the following songs:

● *Hey Jude* (The Beatles)

● *Shape of you* – the underlying ostinato pattern (Ed Sheeran)

● *Under pressure* – bass line (Queen)

● *Twinkle twinkle little star* (traditional)

● *Seven nation army* – bass rhythm (The White Stripes)

● *Hickory dickory dock* (traditional)

● *We will rock you* (Queen)

● *End of time* (Beyoncé)

● *Yellow submarine* (The Beatles)

● *All you need is love* (The Beatles)

● *Bring it all back* (S Club 7)

● *Ticket to ride* (The Beatles)

● *Acapella* – opening rhythm (Kelis)

● *This love* – rhythm of the first line of the chorus (Maroon 5)

Top tip

Only share the lyrics if they are appropriate. Otherwise, keep the rhythm source to yourself.

Taking it further...

Try putting the first lines onto tuned percussion to make original melodies (see Idea 23).

Action numbers **26**

"The children were very quickly better than me!"

This activity helps children develop rhythm and co-ordination.

Age: 7–11

◉ Altogether, in a circle, set up a slow, steady and repeating count of:
1 – 2 – 3 – 4 – 5 – 6, 1 – 2 – 3 – 4 – 5 – 6 …

◉ Choose an action to do on '1', e.g. clap:

clap – 2 – 3 – 4 – 5 – 6 – clap – 2 – 3 – 4 – 5 – 6 …

◉ Once secure, introduce another action, e.g. stamp on 3:

clap – 2 – stamp – 4 – 5 – 6 – clap – 2 – stamp – 4 – 5 – 6 …

◉ If everyone can co-ordinate their movements in time, introduce a further action on 4:

clap – 2 – stamp – stretch – 5 – 6 – clap – 2 – stamp – stretch – 5 – 6 …

◉ Continue adding actions until all the numbers have been replaced by actions.

Develop further, by asking everyone to march around the circle instead of standing still.

◉ Set the marching going first – making sure everyone is marching with their same foot at the same time:

left – right – left – right – left – right …

◉ Introduce the counting:

left – 2 – 3 – 4 – 5 – 6 – left – 2 – 3 – 4 – 5 – 6 …

◉ Then introduce an action for one of the counts as above, to perform whilst marching, e.g.

clap – 2– 3 – 4 – 5 – 6 – clap – 2 – 3 – 4 – 5 – 6 …

◉ Introduce additional actions on the other counts one at a time, ensuring each one is secure before adding the next, e.g.

clap – 2 – hands high – 4 – roll hands 6 – clap – 2 – hands high – 4 – roll hands – 6…

Taking it further...

Encourage children to suggest/introduce different actions that can be achieved whilst still walking to a regular beat.

Bonus idea

The marching version works well when children are moving around school (see Idea 32).

27 Let the children teach

"I get lots of my ideas from working with a local cub group."

Encouraging children to share co-ordination games (passing, clapping or skipping games and songs) learnt on the playground or through after-school organisations, can be a wonderful way to build self-esteem (as well as add to your repertoire). It can be extremely beneficial for EAL children who might introduce activities from their own country/region/culture.

Age: All

Many of the ideas in this book might appear similar to games children play in the playground, or at groups such as brownies, beavers, cubs, etc. This shouldn't be altogether surprising, as many ideas in music sessions were inspired by, or began as children's games.

Children will often have their own rhythmic hand games, passing games, songs and co-ordination games.

Top tip

EAL children, or children from other localities will often have games or songs your class don't know, sometimes with non-English words. Sharing these will not only help raise the self-esteem of the children doing the sharing, but also help children learn to value others' culture and language.

Invite children to teach them to you and the class. They will often have practised a lot and be experts, therefore raising their self-esteem as they demonstrate to others, and act as the teacher.

Furthermore, by acting as the teacher, the child teaching the activty will better understand the skills required.

Other children who might otherwise be reluctant to lead an activity, may feel more confident after seeing their peers have a go.

The noisy old lady 28

"This activity had them giggling with enjoyment. We were able to make links to other areas of the curriculum too."

This activity introduces the musical elements, now called the 'inter-related dimensions of music' (NC 2014) in a fun activity that uses the song *There was an old lady who swallowed a fly*.

Age: 4 –7

Resources: Pictures of fly, spider, bird, cat, dog, cow, horse; a selection of tuned and untuned percussion instruments including sound effect instruments (e.g. Swanee whistle, kazoo); guitar/ukulele (if available)

Start by learning the song together. (You can listen to the song at **dwheway.wikispaces.com/100+ideas+Music**

There was an old lady who swallowed a fly,

I don't know why she swallowed the fly, perhaps she'll die!

There was an old lady who swallowed a spider, that wriggled and jiggled and tickled inside her,

She swallowed the spider to catch the fly, but

I don't know why she swallowed the fly, perhaps she'll die!

There was an old lady who swallowed a bird – how absurd to swallow a bird!

She swallowed the bird to catch the spider …

There was an old lady who swallowed a cat – fancy that, she swallowed a cat!...

There was an old lady who swallowed a dog – what a hog to swallow a dog!...

There was an old lady who swallowed a cow – I don't know how she swallowed a cow!...

There was an old lady who swallowed a horse – she's dead of course!

(An alternative ending is – *she's full of course!*)

> **Top tip**
>
> The 'elements of music' or 'inter-related dimensions' might appear challenging, but they closely relate to the spoken word: we whisper or shout (*dynamics*), talk in a high- or low-pitched voice (*pitch*), drawl or gabble (*tempo*), all speak at once/alone/in unison (*texture*), speak rhythmically (*duration*), speak in rough/posh/silly voices (*timbre*). And *structure* simply means the organisation of sound/phrases.

Next, sing the song again, but ask the children to improvise sounds for each creature, e.g sing, 'There was an old lady who swallowed a fly'; pause for 'bzzzzzzzzzzz' sounds; continue song.

With the class, explore each of the musical elements to create a class performance of the song:

○ Structure: Explain that it is a cumulative song that gets longer with each added animal.

○ Pitch: Notice how the final phrase, 'Perhaps she'll die' moves up in steps.

Per - haps   she'll   die

○ Timbre: Allocate each creature to a group of children and ask them to find instruments and create sounds for their creature.

○ Dynamics: Encourage each group to consider how loudly or quietly to perform their sounds.

○ Duration: Which improvised sounds are longer/shorter? (e.g. long 'bzzzzzzzzzzzzzzzz' sounds; short 'woof' sounds)

○ Texture: Explore ways of performing the piece to create different textures, e.g. as each creature is swallowed their sound continues as the next one is swallowed, etc.

○ Tempo: Decide on a speed to perform the song, e.g. it could start fast and get slower.

Rehearse the song and adapt sounds until you are all happy with it.

Perform your version of the song to a chosen audience (parents, assembly, another class).

Taking it further...

Record only the sounds in sequence. Can another class guess the song?

Bonus idea

Children compose their own piece in which they sequence a set of objects which gets progressively larger, whilst exploring the musical elements.

Name that sound 29

"The class were really quiet and attentive, and came up with some wonderful descriptions."

This activity helps develop attentive, focused listening. Children attempt to locate sounds, and they build a technical language to describe sounds.

Age: 4–7

Ask the children to close their eyes and be as quiet as possible, and to ignore your movements around the room.

Move around the room finding two or three sounds to make within the classroom environment (such as rattling a pencil pot, turning a tap on or off, moving a chair, flipping paper on a flip chart, sliding the waste bin gently along, gliding a hand in gentle sweeps across a poster, and so on).

Ask the children to open their eyes, and discuss the sounds:

❍ Can anyone describe the first sound you made?

❍ Can children point in the direction it came from?

❍ Can children find good words to describe the sound (real or invented words)?

❍ Can children say how long the sound lasted, how loud it was, how it made them feel?

❍ Can they say how they think you made the sound – being as specific as possible (e.g. if they identified you were gliding your hand across paper, which part of your hand?)

❍ Can they identify the direction and source of the sound?

Repeat for the other sounds you made.

Invite individuals to find a sound. Allow them time to decide on a sound, or ask them to think what they might do for the next time you play this game.

Top tip

Think ahead about what sounds you can find around the classroom before playing the game.

Taking it further...

Make recordings from a particular location (e.g. in town, in the woods, on holiday, around the house). Back in the classroom ask children to identify the sounds.

30 Singing the register

"I can't believe how much the children love this activity — they are always asking to do it!"

This activity often surprises teachers, as the children enjoy it so much and ask for it time and time again. It is a simple way to help children pitch notes accurately as it uses a limited pitch range and number of notes, allowing children to focus on emulating the pitch.

Top tip

Remember that a comfortable pitch for you may not be comfortable for the children. Listen to their responses. If they tend to respond at a lower or higher pitch, try to adjust your pitch accordingly to match the 'class pitch'.

Taking it further...

Try fitting the full name of the child to the melody. You will need to adapt the rhythm and tempo accordingly.

Bonus idea

Children enjoy thinking up responses for children who are absent (occasionally revealing a confidence – for example if the child is 'skiving').

Age: 6+

Instead of saying the register, it is sung using a simple two-note melody (the same interval as a ding-dong doorbell, or when you call, 'cooeee!' – see Idea 7).

Find a comfortable starting pitch and sing 'Is [child's name] here today?' using the two pitches as shown:

Upper note: *Is   here   to -*

Lower note: *[child's name]   day?*

Go through the register. The children reply using the same melody:

Upper note: *Yes   here   to -*

Lower note: *I'm   day.*

Children's quality of response can be very varied (spoken, sung on a monotone, sung at a different pitch to you and/or the other children). Don't draw attention to this during this quick and fun activity, but instead you might note children who would benefit from further support, for example when singing in music lessons.

Tidy-up time

"We always clear away now to music. The children love it, and are very good at finishing before the music ends."

Clearing away in a given time develops a sense of time in the children. By using a piece of music, they respond to, and develop their knowledge of the piece through repeated listening. Depending on the selected piece, they might also respond with movement to the piece.

Age: 4–7

Resources: A recording of a tune the children enjoy

Children enjoy clearing away to music, and the music dictates a set time by which everyone should be cleared away and ready.

A commonly-used tune for younger children is *Hi ho, hi ho, it's off to work we go* from the Disney film *Snow White*. Other good clearing away music includes:

● *Flight of the bumble bee* by Rimsky-Korsakov

● *Troika* by Prokofiev

● *Theme from Mission: Impossible* by Lalo Schifrin

● *Yakety Sax* by Boots Randolph and James Rich

● *Peter Gunn* by Henry Mancini

Top tip

Try to make this activity feel enjoyable, and let the music guide the children. It would be sad if children associated a piece of music with a stressful event.

Taking it further...

In time, see if the children respond as soon as the music begins, possibly without any instruction from you!

32 Keep 'em moving, keep 'em grooving

"The children sing all the time now — when they are changing for PE, when they go on school trips..."

This idea is about building a bank of simple songs and rhythm games to use whenever possible during the school day. It is excellent for developing memory, pitch matching, rhythm skills and vocal confidence.

Age: 6–9

Find appropriate opportunities to sing songs or play rhythm games during the school day (e.g. when on playground duty; lining up; filler activities; moving round the school; bus journeys:

Top tip

There are many examples of easy songs and games in this book. The Internet is also a great source: search for 'fun songs', 'campfire songs', 'circle time songs'; 'call and response songs' – and of course, invite the children to share songs and games that they know (see Idea 27).

Taking it further...

Invite the children to write their own songs or rhythm games – concentrating on the rhythm and rhyme of the words. They could write their own melodies too.

◑ Sing when moving around the school: Depending on where they are going, the children may be in a single line or walking in pairs – sing songs as you move from place to place. Good examples to start with are: *On top of spaghetti*; *The bear went over the mountain*; *This old man*; *One man went to mow*; *Everywhere you go*, etc.

◑ Sing on the bus when going on school trips: Use the same bank of songs on the bus – singing songs can distract them from feeling sick or calm them down after exciting events.

◑ Warm-ups and filler activities: Teach rhythm games and short simple songs as warm-ups or filler activities – as well as being fun, they are excellent for getting children focused. Some good ones to start with are: *Animal ostinati*, *Let's go disco-dancing*, *Singing tennis* and *Rhythms for attention* (see Ideas 9, 17, 22 and 25).

Singing together when moving around the school or going on a school trip helps build the social cohesion of a school community. Over time you will find that children will sing spontaneously and may create their own versions!

"Are there other ways I can develop music in my class?"

Music needn't just take place in curriculum slots. 'Music areas' mirror other areas where children can explore, or continue work introduced during lessons.

How can I utilise a music area?

- listening posts with headphones – listening to music, including their own compositions
- iPads – developing knowledge of music apps
- a selection of tuned and untuned percussion – to explore sound, melody and accompaniment
- iPads or PCs – researching an artist, composer, an interest in a musical instrument, etc.
- photos, pictures, graphic scores and notations – to follow up activities introduced in music lessons.

Won't it be a disturbance to other children?

Like any other area, children should develop respect for the resources, and other children engaged elsewhere. Using soft beaters and quieter percussion helps.

I can see how it would work in an Early Years setting, but what about with older children?

Time spent in a music area counts towards music time, so instead of an hour-long music lesson you could have a 20-minute lesson ... up by groups in the music area during the week. Children ... the subsequent lesson with ideas and ready for next steps.

... take time – supervising an ... al area in the classroom?

However, children can often pursue ... that require very little adult support. ...-interaction activities might include ...reas, finishing creative work, project ... ny computer apps/programs. These ... can allow the teacher/other adult to ... high-interaction activities.

> **Top tip**
>
> Allow older children to maintain the music area. Suggest an idea – they will often enjoy the responsibility to develop the idea and decorate the area.

36 What have we done today?

"This is a lovely way to get children to reflect on their day"

This idea uses the well-known tune **Polly put the kettle on** with new words that encourage children to reflect on their day. It is best sung close to home time so they can sing it to the person who comes to collect them.

Top tip

If any child is reluctant to sing in response, still focus on them and sing alongside them or for them.

Taking it further...

Sing the song earlier in the day using the words: 'What will (Phi-llip) do today?' To which the child responds with what he/she would like to do, e.g. 'I'll play in the sand.' (This, of course, might alert you to the fact that Phillip is spending rather a lot of time in the sand!)

Age: 3–5

All sit in a circle for this activity.

● Ask the children to think of something they have done today that they enjoyed or that was important or memorable in some way.

● Chose a child to focus on and sing (to the tune of *Polly put the kettle on*):

Teacher: *What has (Phi-llip) done today?*

  What has (Phi-llip) done today?

  What has (Phi-llip) done today?

(Pause for child's response)

Child: *I've played in the sand.*

● Comment on this, then sing again choosing a different child.

● Encourage children to join in with you in the first three phrases each time.

Tuned percussion play 37

"The sounds are quite hypnotic and very relaxing."

Here children develop simple improvisation skills creating short repeating melodies. It is a very valuable activity – and should be allowed to progress over a lengthy period of time (10–20 minutes). It can provide a very active and focused start to a morning or afternoon.

Age: 6+

Resources: Lots of tuned percussion and beaters

This idea works well as a warm-up for Idea 23. You will need a large space. Arrange all your tuned percussion in a large circle, with children seated behind the percussion facing into the circle.

- Ask all the children to invent a short melody that they can play repeatedly on their tuned percussion. Let children all play at the same time. Don't worry if the first few times they attempt this activity they don't reflect on the overall sound.
- If children struggle to find a repeating melody, give them a short rhythm such as 'Simple Simon met a pie-man' (see Idea 23).
- Identify and mentally select a child who appears confident and is managing a repeated melody. (Sometimes if there's a lot of sound, you might need to observe, rather than hear this.)
- Use a hand 'stop' sign to stop individual children playing until only the child you mentally selected is playing.
- Ask children to listen carefully to that child.
- Bring children back in individually/in sections. They should try and fit their existing or new patterns to the selected child.
- Identify a new child and repeat the process.

Top tip

Using felt beaters as opposed to hard plastic or wood on xylophones will create a gentler sound. Ensure every child has a beater for each hand, as this helps develop co-ordination.

Taking it further...

Ask other children to take your place as conductor for 30 seconds or so. Over time, encourage children to listen more and more carefully to others, and to try to ensure their melodies fit together well, without being identical.

Bonus idea

An adult modelling playing at half or double speed can encourage children to consider changing the duration of their notes.

38 Pitch cards

"Why didn't we do this when I was at school?"

Here, pitch notation is pared back, making creating and playing melodies more accessible. It also helps children who subsequently go on to learn stave notation (e.g. through instrumental lessons).

Age: 5+

Resources: Sets of pitch cards (and blank stave cards for age 7+); a selection of tuned percussion; paper and pencils/felt tips

Ages 5–6

Make a set of the following four pitch cards:

Top tip

The pitches don't need to be specific. As long as one pitch is relatively high compared to the other in the two dot cards, and there are three distinctly different pitches for the three dot cards, that is fine. As children's listening awareness develops, the pitches can be brought closer together.

Explain that the two dots represent pitch. The higher dot is for a higher pitch. Play one of the cards using tuned percussion, e.g. high–low (card 1). Can they identify which card you played?

Encourage children to explore the cards themselves.

● They test each other in pairs with high and low bars.

● They develop this idea by playing a sequence of two or three cards for their partner to identify, e.g. 'My partner played card 1 then card 3 then card 2':

● Once children are confident, hand out strips of paper for them to create their own longer sequences from which they play, e.g.

Age 7+

Extend the idea using three different pitches: high, medium and low. Make a set of four pitch cards using any combination of the three pitches, e.g.

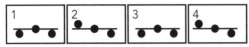

Introduce the pitch cards and let the children explore, using them as described above.

They choose any three notes on their tuned percussion and create sequences using the four cards in any order.

Some children will play the sequences as notes of equal value (sounding like a waltz beat) but most are likely to play a rhythm in each bar of 'short-short-long' beats.

Either way, discuss how children might demonstrate a longer beat.

A good solution (as it links well with stave notation) is by leaving each last beat in the bar 'open'.

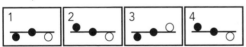

Taking it further...

Leave sets of pitch cards (and blank stave cards) with tuned percussion in a music area for children to continue exploring during the week.

39 Melodic gap fill

"Improvisation is an important part of music and leads well into composition."

Top tip

If resources are limited, place one xylophone in the circle. Children take turns to come to the xylophone to improvise – everyone else maintains the rhythm by clapping. Encourage children to hold a beater in each hand when they play.

Taking it further...

Give children access to a xylophone in the classroom after the lesson (e.g. in a music area) to rehearse what they might play the next time you do this activity.

Bonus idea

Repeat the activity using voices: everyone sings an agreed melody (perhaps one of the children's improvised melodies). Each child then fills the gap with a sung improvisation.

This activity can provide a calm and relaxing part to the day. It develops children's co-ordination, listening and improvisation skills.

Age: 7–11

Resources: Lots of tuned percussion (pentatonic notes C D E G A) and beaters, ideally one instrument between two children

Sit the children in a large circle with tuned percussion in front of them. Allow plenty of time for this activity (e.g. 20 minutes).

● Everyone plays together to a repeating count of eight beats. They might simply play repeated notes, or find a simple pattern of two or three notes.

● Stop all the children playing, then count aloud to eight in the silence.

● After eight, they all start again. Repeat this process until they can all stop (rest) and start together.

● Now, children will take turns around the circle to fill the quiet gap.

● Repeat the playing to a count of eight, then everyone stops except the first child in the circle, who improvises a melodic 'fill'. Depending on ability and confidence this could be anything from a two-note melody to a complex melody – but it shouldn't exceed eight beats.

● Repeat, with the next child in the circle filling the gap, and so on round the circle.

● Don't worry if some children don't play very much – comment positively on any effort they make.

"The conductor improvisation worked well because there was no 'wrong' answer."

This idea builds on Puppet play (Idea 12). Children take turns being the 'Maestro' – conducting using hand and body gestures to direct sound responses from the rest of the class playing instruments.

Age: 7–11

Resources: At least one soundmaker per child, which might be classroom percussion or even instruments children are learning beyond the classroom

All sit in a horseshoe arrangement with the teacher in the gap.

● Begin by showing children that when your hands are by your side they should be silent, but when your hands are in the air they play.

● Remind the children they can play loudly – but to be careful not to damage the instruments (see Idea 12).

● Try a few test gestures to ensure the children understand and can respond accordingly, e.g. practise all starting and stopping.

● Develop the conducting using different hand movements, e.g.

▸ gradually rising/falling hands for louder/ quieter

▸ roly-poly hands for faster/slower tempo;

▸ left hand/right hand to direct the left/right sides of the circle to play

▸ rhythmic hand movements for rhythmic playing.

● Invite children to take your place as 'maestro', finding ways to control the sounds (a form of improvisation).

Top tip

Let nearby teachers know there will be some periods of noise coming from your teaching area!

Taking it further...

Divide children into smaller groups, each with their own, interchangeable, 'maestro'. Each 'maestro' should be encouraged to think about ways to start and stop individual children as well as shape the sounds to affect the texture of their piece.

Bonus idea

Playing with hands rather than beaters wherever possible can avoid accidental damage.

41 Sound chance

"Such a simple idea — with endless permutations."

Children use 'sound chance' cards to create different structures and textures.

Age: 7–11

Resources: Multiple 'sound chance' cards; lots of percussion/other instruments

Create a set of 'sound chance' cards – cards with musical ideas written on them in words. They can be anything you like – to do with pitch, dynamics, layering sounds, rhythm, structure, etc. For example:

a sudden loud sound	a low, hard, repeating sound
loud sounds gradually getting quieter until – silence	a glissando (slide) from low to high
clusters of high-pitched sounds	lots of very quiet silvery sounds
everyone playing as rapidly as possible	hard, brittle sounds followed by very soft sounds
everyone plays – then sounds drop out one by one	one person indicates a period of about five seconds of silence

each person counts in their heads to a different number between one and eight then plays a sound (repeat three times)

single very long sounds

Taking it further...

Leave some blank cards so children can write their own ideas.

Bonus idea !

Ask children to arrange the cards so that sometimes two cards are played at the same time.

Children work in groups of four to six with a set of instruments each. Deal out a set of cards to each group. The children explore and interpret the random sequence.

Riff my rhythm 42

"Once children realised listening and watching was important, they focused and kept their riffs in time."

Children invent a four-beat repeating rhythm pattern (ostinato or 'riff') and maintain their part within a rhythmic ensemble.

Age: 7–11

Resources: Small hand-held percussion, e.g. claves or maracas (and body percussion)

● Set a steady beat of 4, '1 2 3 4' tapping thighs. Children join in.

● Once the beat is established, emphasise the count of four as an introduction, and invite each child in turn to improvise a four-beat rhythm pattern on body percussion. They repeat their pattern over and over as more children join in, until a given 'stop' signal. Suggest they use a word pattern to generate their rhythm, e.g. a short phrase, children's names (see Idea 3), favourite food, etc. Transfer to untuned percussion.

1	2	3	+	4
Craig	Craig	Ra	- vi	Craig ...

or

1	+	2	+	3	+	4
I	can	play	a	four-beat	riff	...

● It may take several attempts and a bit of practise to keep the ensemble together.

● When everyone is playing together, direct individuals to join in or stop their riffs, creating different textures (layers).

● Invite individuals to be the conductor/leader and to set the tempo and direct the other children when to start and stop their riffs.

43 Sound and silence

"The quiet parts make the other sounds so dramatic. I'm going to use this idea in drama."

Silence is an integral element of music – used to great effect by most composers to change the mood of a piece and add emphasis. In this idea, children create simple sequences incorporating silence or very quiet sounds to contrast with other parts of the sequence.

Age: 7–11

Taking it further...

Return to other activities the children have tried, and consider whether a silence could be incorporated and how this might affect the piece. For example, in 'Tuned percussion play' (Idea 37), include a signal for all to stop playing and be as quiet as possible. Reflect on how long a silence can be to remain effective.

Bonus idea

Research the piece 4'33" by the 20th century composer, John Cage. You might even watch a performance on YouTube. Is the performance totally silent? Research Cage's intentions for this piece.

Resources: Body percussion, classroom percussion and other instruments/soundmakers

● Standing in a circle, all rub hands gently. Keep going, getting quieter and quieter until the sound is barely audible, if possible so quiet that no one is quite sure if there is any sound.

● Now stop and value the stillness. But is it completely quiet? Sound will intrude from within and beyond the classroom. However, these are probably sounds we can't control. (Perhaps take a few seconds to identify the sounds.)

● Next, take up instruments and explain that, on a given signal, everyone will make the loudest, shortest sound they can (being careful not to damage the instruments). Children may need to stop the sound or hold their instrument in a certain way to ensure the sound is very short (this isn't always easy).

● You, or a confident child, now create a sequence of loud sounds and silences by directing the class using agreed signals, (hand signs, stepping into and out of a hoop, dancing/stopping, etc.)

● Reflect on the silences. Are they effective and if so, how? How long can a silence be to remain effective? Could a piece be just silence?

"This idea has so many links across the curriculum."

Here, children explore vocal sounds for pictures, which are then arranged into simple sequences. Through this activity children learn that they can create their own structures including repeated sounds, and create short themed compositions.

Age: 4–6

Resources: Two or three pictures/photographs to do with a chosen theme (e.g. the seaside, minibeasts, pets, etc.) – three copies of each

All sit in a large circle for this activity:

● Hold up one of the cards (e.g. seagulls) and ask children to suggest vocal sounds to represent the picture.

● Children decide on a favourite sound of a few seconds for that particular picture and practise it together – then set the card to one side.

● Hold up the second picture (e.g. shingle on the beach), and repeat the above.

● Place the two cards on the floor in front of you. Tell the children you'd like them to make the sound for whichever picture you point to.

● Now point to each picture randomly to make a short sequence, occasionally pointing to the same picture twice, e.g.

seagulls – shingle – seagulls – shingle – shingle

● Afterwards, see if any of the children can recall your sequence.

● Did they notice you pointing twice in succession to one of the pictures?

● Repeat the ideas above – now introducing a third card (e.g. children splashing in the waves).

● Finally, you can introduce more complex sequences, e.g.

seagulls – shingle – splashing – seagulls – shingle

Taking it further...

Place the cards in the music area, so that children can choose to go to the area to create their own sequences.

Bonus idea

Invite a volunteer to come and make a short pattern by walking/pointing to each picture in a sequence. (Very young children might need stopping after a little while – or they might continue until home time!)

45 Colour and sound

"How can you make a colour into a sound? What does green sound like then?"

A photograph of a real landscape is used here to introduce composing from a non-musical starting point. Children are challenged to think differently and use sound as a metaphor. Thinking together about how to represent green, brown or black in sound heightens aural discrimination and creativity.

Age: 8–11

Resources: a photograph of a large, colourful landscape projected on an interactive whiteboard; a selection of tuned and untuned instruments

Display the landscape photograph. Make sure there are about six major colours that are well-represented in the photograph.

○ Ask children what colours they can see in the photograph and note them down.

○ Divide the class into six groups of five or six and allocate one colour to each group. They should use voices and instruments to agree on and produce a sound that will in some way represent 'their' colour.

○ After five to ten minutes of experimentation, ask each group to 'play their colour'.

○ Discuss ways to help refine their music (e.g. prolonging or varying their sound; more attention to dynamics and timbre).

○ Now use a pointer to 'read' across the landscape photograph, slowly moving from left to right, children playing the colours as they arise.

○ When two or three colours occur together then all sounds should occur at once (creating a thicker texture).

Top tip

Using a number of contrasting colours encourages synaesthetic thinking, translating something seen into something heard. There are no wrong answers.

Taking it further...

Groups compose to other pictures (a castle or other building in a setting; a seascape; a sunset or an abstract painting). Encourage the children to think about where silences could be inserted and where they could repeat or make a deliberate contrast using dynamics and different textures.

Bonus idea

Children create a spectrum of colour (e.g. dark red to pale pink) interpreted in sound.

Sounds from stories 46

"I can think of lots of books in our setting that I can use for this activity."

Traditional stories and other Early Years stories often have words suggestive of sound, mood or actions, and they may have repeating phrases. Children join in with vocal sounds/repeating phrases as you read the story.

Age: 4–5

Resources: Selection of tuned and untuned percussion and other soundmakers

This activity uses *The three little pigs*, but the idea can easily be adapted to other stories.

❍ Relate *The three little pigs*, pausing for children to make sounds on words/phrases that prompt sounds (e.g. 'huff', 'puff', pigs squealing, building with straw/wood/brick and repeated phrases such as 'No, No, by the hair on my chinny chin chin', etc.).

❍ Children explore soundmakers and percussion to enhance their sounds, e.g. by having: a range of instruments for children to explore in a music area; a circuit of soundmakers in hoops, which groups explore for a few minutes; a soundmaker each.

❍ Children make sounds for each character/event during the story. They choose one character/event for which they feel their soundmaker is best, and respond to the cues as the story is retold. Ideas for using soundmakers include:

Huffing and puffing: ocean drum tipped from side to side.

Pigs: vocal squeaks.

Wolf: vocal roars.

Running: any regular tapping rhythm.

Building with straw: brushes drawn across drums, cabasas.

Building with wood: soft tapping wood sounds such as woodblocks, two-tone blocks, claves.

Building with bricks: hard tapping wood sounds.

Spoken repeating phrases of the wolf and the pigs.

Taking it further...

Other story ideas include: *We're going on a bear hunt* (Michael Rosen); *Goodnight owl* (Pat Hutchins), *Where the wild things are* (Maurice Sendak); *Peace at last* (Jill Murphy).

47 Sound journeys

"You could link this with so many different themes."

Children explore sound sources to respond to a real or imaginary journey. For younger children the characters and events might simply act as a cue to play, whereas older children can develop sounds, rhythms, melodies and accompaniments as representations.

Age: All (depending on approach)

Resources: A selection of tuned and untuned percussion instruments; the 'journey' displayed on a whiteboard using four or five representative pictures, each linked by a line

The focus of this activity is a 'journey'. It can be any journey. In the example below, the theme is a nature walk. This might be an imagined walk, or possibly based on an actual outdoor activity with the children. The journey might be displayed using pictures of the following:

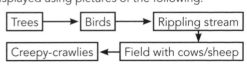

Ask children to explore sets of instruments and other sound sources to find sounds to complement each stage of the journey. This might be done in groups, with each group responsible for one part of the journey. In the above example, the children might choose:

○ Trees – vocal sounds; gently rubbing hands; rustled/flapped/scrunched paper sounds

○ Birds – vocal tweets and whistles

○ Rippling stream – vocal gurgling sounds; sliding sounds on glockenspiels

○ Field with cows and/or sheep – vocal mooing/baa-ing

○ Creepy-crawlies – fingers crawling; fast, scraped guiros; click clacks.

Perform the journey. You point to the pictures and the children respond by making the sounds for the events in the journey as each is approached, then fading as you move on.

Discuss other ways to make your sound journey.

Bonus idea

Children explore their rhythms on tuned percussion to develop simple melodies. Older children could explore instruments they are learning, as well as classroom percussion, voices and body percussion.

Graphic scores

"This was a huge hit in my class!"

Children create their own symbols to represent sounds and create simple compositions.

Age: 6+

Resources: A selection of different soundmakers; paper and crayons

Demonstrate how to create some simple symbol cards to represent sounds on percussion, e.g. three vertical lines for tapping claves three times; a wavy line for shaking a tambourine and getting quieter; a swirl to show swirling a hand round the skin of a drum.

Play the sounds to the children, then ask if they can say which symbol card went with which sound.

Encourage the children to explore the different soundmakers and find a sound for which they create their own symbol. Share some examples with the other children.

Divide the class into small groups and ask each group to combine their individual sounds and symbols into a pattern or sequence. They perform their combined sequences to the rest of the class.

Discuss with the children how they might alter their symbols to demonstrate loud and quiet (dynamics), hard and soft (timbre), long and short sounds (duration), and high and low (pitch) if using tuned percussion.

Top tip

Encourage the children to use body sounds and found sounds as well as classroom instruments.

Taking it further...

Ask children how they might show two or more instruments playing at the same time.

Bonus idea

Groups create sequences, and then invite another group to interpret their graphic score.

49 Structurally sound

"I wish I'd done this when I was young, I'd have understood GCSE music much better!"

This idea uses children's own compositions to learn about form and structure. They use letters of the alphabet as naming devices.

Age: 6+ (although initial ideas can be shared with quite young children)

You may have encountered the convention of using capital letters to identify structure in music, e.g. ABACADA (rondo form). This activity helps explain how this works and how easy it is to use.

● Choose any previously-composed short group pieces.

● Name the groups: group A, group B, group C and so on.

● The class decides on an order for each group to play their piece to create a longer class piece (e.g. a simple structure with six groups would be A B C D E F).

● Explore different ways of structuring the piece, including some groups playing more than once.

● Explore some common musical structures:

Two groups (two composed sections)

ABABAB and so on – often used for hymn or folk song structures: verse, chorus, verse, chorus, verse, chorus, and so on

AB – known as binary form (classical music)

ABA – known as ternary form (classical music)

Three groups (three composed sections)

ABABCB – often used in pop or folk songs: verse, chorus, verse, chorus, middle 8 (or instrumental), chorus

Four groups (four composed sections)

ABABCD – often used in pop or folk songs: verse, chorus, verse, chorus, middle 8 (or instrumental), coda (ending)

ABACADA and so on – known as rondo form (classical music)

Taking it further...

Try identifying the structures of other music, e.g. as outlined in Idea 61.

Bonus idea

Listen to some pop or folk music, and identify the different sections: verse, chorus, middle 8 section (often instrumental, solo spot or new words), and the coda (the end of the piece which might repeat a chorus and fade and/or be slightly different to the rest of the song).

Mood cards 50

"I was surprised how little the groups needed my help to create their music."

Teachers are often surprised at how easily children can respond to a given mood or emotion through their own short compositions. In this activity children work in groups to find sounds to represent a mood word, and others then identify the mood.

Age: 7–11

Resources: Mood cards with different moods (such as 'happy', 'sad', 'busy', 'sleepy', 'scary', 'bored', etc.); a selection of different soundmakers (older children could bring in their own instruments to add to the sound possibilities)

Divide the class into groups of around six children. Give each group a name.

⦿ Give each group a mood card, which they should keep secret from the other groups.

⦿ Explain that each group will interpret their mood in a short piece of music around 15 to 20 seconds in length.

⦿ Allow up to five minutes for the children to explore, then create their pieces. Make sure they think about how their music will start and finish.

⦿ Display all the group mood words together in a random order (e.g. on the whiteboard).

⦿ Ask the first group to play their music – and ask the other children if they can identify the mood from the list.

⦿ Children vote on their choice – write the group name next to that word. (Tell the children they are allowed to change their mind later – before the final 'reveal').

⦿ Once all the groups have played, and the moods of each piece have been decided, it is time to see how accurate the voters were.

Taking it further...

Listen again to one or more of the pieces as a class, asking children not in the group to suggest ideas for more closely matching the mood. Alternatively, pair groups together to advise each other how to develop their music further.

Bonus idea

Create a simple sequence for all the groups to play, such as group A, group B, group C... (see Idea 49). Ask the children to suggest alternative mood sequences.

51 Haiku

"Turning a poem into music helped me understand what creativity is — and what fun it is too."

Turning a simple poem like a haiku into music can help children discover their own musical creativity. Using the three-line structure and the simply expressed ideas of the haiku form, children can experiment with all the dimensions of music.

Age: 8–11

Resources: a sheet of A4 paper with blanks for the poem and enough space for experimentation with words; a wide range of classroom instruments

Do not tell children this is a music lesson at first.

○ Ask each child to pick up something very small and insignificant in the environment around them.

○ Remind them how to write a haiku and give them five minutes to write one about their object.

Top tip

You will need to have explained the idea of a Japanese haiku poem. They have exactly 17 syllables in just three lines: one of 5 syllables, one of 7 and the last of 5. The first line draws attention to a tiny aspect of the environment (e.g. a leaf, petal, hair or screwed-up crisp packet); the second line describes it in poetic form; the last line asks a deep question or makes some profound statement about it.

HAIKU – a seventeen syllable poem
_ _ _ _ _ **(5)**
_ _ _ _ _ _ _ **(7)**
_ _ _ _ _ **(5)**

Gather children into groups of five or six to share their haikus with each other and ask them to choose one they agree would be best set to music.

Give each group the following instructions:

○ Their music must be one minute long.

○ All members of the group must play or speak in it.

○ It should somehow 'sound' like the object the poem is about.

○ It must represent the three lines of the poem.

The children may need some help to brainstorm ideas before they attempt to make the music last for one minute, e.g.

○ sing the chosen poem several times

○ make it into a round

○ pick out key words and shout them, whisper them lots of times or just illustrate them in sound

○ possibly accompany the dramatic speaking of the poem with atmospheric sounds

○ turn the poem into sound only (no words)

○ play with the sounds of the words in any other way they like.

Ask groups to work together and be as creative as they can with sound. Visit each composing group to listen in to ideas. Congratulate children on original, arresting and imaginative ideas with the words. Encourage them to refine ideas, use periods of silence, consider dynamics, pitch, timbre, etc.

After 10 to 15 minutes invite each group to perform their work in progress. They then refine their ideas before performing their group pieces a second time.

Taking it further...

Involve all children in supportive assessment – congratulating each group on two or three specific aspects of the compositions and asking one question that might make the composing group think.

Bonus idea

Make a complete performance of the session by projecting images, performing the basic poems, filming the process of turning them into music and presenting the musical haikus to another class.

52 Sound aware

"I realise listening is such an important part of being musical."

Taking time throughout the day to be calm and listen carefully is really important for children, and can have knock-on effects across the curriculum. Being aware of our surroundings and learning to identify and describe sounds is an important aspect of developing musically.

Age: 5+

Resources: A selection of percussion instruments and other sound sources to follow up the listening activity

Top tip

This idea links well with Ideas 44, 47 and 70.

Taking it further...

Create simple sequences of these sounds for short compositions.

Bonus idea

Utilise mobile technology to record sounds in the environment. These can then be used to create a sound collage (using apps such as **Music Mike Create** or programs such as **Audacity** – see Ideas 81–82).

● At various times during the day, and where possible in different places (such as on school visits or field trips), encourage the children to close their eyes, relax (even lie down if appropriate) and listen to the sounds around them for about 30 seconds.

● Ask the children to relate what sounds they heard.

● Were there sounds that you noticed that the children appeared unaware of (perhaps common/everyday sounds they shut out, such as a humming radiator or a nearby motorway, etc.)?

● Make a note of some of the sounds the children noticed, and when back in the classroom, explore and try to replicate the sounds vocally, or using percussion or other soundmakers.

Mirror manouevre

"I'm amazed at how quickly kids 'get' this idea."

Children respond to beat in recorded music using mirroring and co-ordination games. This activity encourages communication by listening, sharing, turn-taking and carefully copying the rhythms, movements and sounds that a partner makes.

Age: 5–7 (particularly good for children with SEND)

Resources: recorded music; squares of lycra or stretchy strips ('therabands') or a mini trampoline or raised board that vibrates under the weight of a child lying on it; a selection of tuned percussion instruments (optional)

Mirror game

Choose a piece of recorded music with a strong beat (e.g. pop songs, marches, dance tracks, etc.). Children sit in pairs opposite each other.

❍ Play the music extract, and ask one of each pair to respond to the music either with clapping or moving, following the beat.

❍ The first child indicates to the second when to join in by mirroring their movements.

❍ Invite pairs to demonstrate their responses in turns to the class. Encourage the audience to evaluate the performance with positive comments and possible points for improvement.

Feel the beat game

Especially effective for children with limited movement.

❍ Share a stretchy strip (a 'theraband') or square of lycra between the two children in a pair.

❍ Instead of mirroring their partner's actions, the second child physically feels the beat from their partner through the lycra.

❍ Alternatively, a group of children could surround a child lying on a trampoline or a raised board that can vibrate. These children can tap out a rhythm on the edge of the trampoline or board for the child in the centre to feel movement through it.

Taking it further...

After mirroring simple movements, turn off the recorded music and introduce more complex sounds and rhythms with more able children. Then ask pairs of children to mirror sounds and rhythms with each other on tuned instruments.

54 Hidden sounds

"This helps children explore and play sounds."

A selection of 'sounds' are hidden from the children. They have to listen carefully to identify which sound is being played.

Age: 3–6

Taking it further...

Increase the challenge by including more pairs of instruments. The child secretly playing could play two different sounds and invite two children to identify the sounds by playing them in the centre of the circle.

Bonus idea

Increase the challenge further by choosing a set of similar sounding percussion (e.g. claves and woodblocks) so the children have to listen very carefully to match the sounds.

Resources: A selection of untuned percussion – two of each instrument (e.g. two maracas, two claves and two drums)

All in a circle for this activity.

❍ Introduce the instruments to be played and show how there are two of each.

❍ Place one of each instrument in the centre of the circle and hide the others.

❍ Invite a child to secretly play one of the hidden instruments.

❍ Ask a volunteer to work out which instrument was playing and play its partner in the centre of the circle (e.g. if they heard claves, they play the claves in the circle).

❍ Ask other children to agree whether the volunteer chose the correct sound.

❍ Continue with other children.

Catch the beat

"I'd never thought of catching as being a musical skill!"

This idea combines PE and music to develop beat, and throwing and catching skills. It develops the skill of anticipating the beat as well as feeling the beat.

Age: 7–11

Resources: Balls, beanbags or hoops; a drum or tambour, and possibly a recording of music with a slow beat (such as the Barcarolle from 'The tales of Hoffman' by Offenbach)

● Start by asking children to throw and catch a ball, beanbag or hoop to each other in pairs.

● Next, set a very slow, steady beat on the tambour and ask the children to try to catch on the beat of a tambour. This means the child throwing has to anticipate the next beat, to ensure the object is thrown in time for their partner to catch on the beat (not easy). The catcher must try and time the catch so that their hands come together exactly on the beat.

● Try forming groups of four and asking children to pass the ball/beanbag/hoop around/across the group.

● Play a piece of recorded music with a strong, slow beat: the first child throws on the first beat, their partner catches on next beat, and so on.

Top tip

If you find it difficult to provide a slow beat on a tambour, find an online metronome and set the speed to 40 beats per minute (bpm) or slower.

Taking it further...

Challenge children to think of other ways of passing between them, including rolling, passing two objects at the same time (each throwing to their partner), getting the ball to bounce on the beat between partners, etc.

56 What's my line?

"It makes you really listen to the music and look for smaller details."

Children listen carefully to short music extracts. They develop a technical vocabulary, choosing the best-fit description, developing words and phrases relating to musical elements, source of the music (country/region), time and/or musical era, mood of the music, and possibly the purpose of the music.

Age: 6–11

Resources: Displays of the music descriptions below (simple descriptions for younger children or more advanced descriptions for older children); recording of *Dance of the Sugar Plum Fairy* by Tchaikovsky

Display the two descriptions while the children listen to the recording. Ask them to decide which description fits best.

Simple descriptions (younger children)

> 1. The music starts with gentle plucking sounds, then is quite twinkly. It isn't very loud. It has a low sound as well. It is meant to be a fairy dancing.

> 2. The music is cheerful. It has a bouncy rhythm. It is meant to be of baby elephants walking.

Top tip

The false description is for *Baby elephant walk* by Mancini (original orchestration). You could repeat the activity playing that recording instead of *Dance of the Sugar Plum Fairy* with another class.

Advanced descriptions (older children)

1. The music begins with gently plucked strings. After a short time, a celesta plays the melody – which is very high in pitch and sounds like tiny bells or tapped glasses. The tempo is quite slow, more like a light, gentle dance. A low-pitched instrument (bass clarinet) plays a descending phrase. This is played later on by two higher clarinets, both contrasting with the high pitch of the celesta. The music was written for a ballet.

2. After a short introduction on a calliope (type of riverboat or circus organ) the music has a boogie-woogie rhythm, with brass and woodwind instruments playing the accompaniment. There is also a drum kit. Clarinet and piccolo alternate playing a jolly melody – joined by a glockenspiel. As the piece continues it gets jazzier, with raucous brass and slightly more complex melodies, before returning to the earlier simpler melodies.

Bonus idea !

Invite children to write their own descriptions of the music, rather than accept the ones given here, e.g. 'This music made me feel _____. The _____ instrument(s) was like _____. When the _____ played, it made me think of _____.'

57 Exploring vocal sounds

"This is a good way to allow experimentation, making different sounds with percussion."

The voice is the most versatile of all instruments. In this idea, children explore their vocal sounds. These could be: imitative (animals, characters, objects); voluntary and non-voluntary (coughs, sneezes); languages; exclamations; showing off (hoots, whistles, etc.); and of course sung items, including hums, ahhs, etc.

Age: 6–11

Everyone is in a circle. Set the ball rolling with your own sound.

- One by one, going round the circle, the children improvise a single sound they can make vocally, which should be unique to them.
- Sometimes a child might say something like: 'I don't know what to do', or 'Ummm?' which are, of course, vocal sounds. Consider telling them that is now their sound, which they will need to use during the game.
- If children don't have any ideas, suggest a theme such as farmyard animals, or involuntary sounds (e.g. coughs, sneezes).
- If two sounds are too alike, encourage the second child to think of something different.
- Practise going round the circle a few times until children are confident producing their sounds in order.

Sound sequence

- Repeat the activity again, this time with children's eyes closed. Everyone listens carefully for the sound immediately preceding theirs, which is their cue to make their own sound.
- Make a note of the final sound in the sequence, and which child made it.
- Then, ask the children to change positions in the circle and repeat the activity with closed eyes again.
- Begin the sequence as before with your sound. The sequence should remain the same, the sounds now bouncing around and across the circle until the final sound in the sequence.
- Repeat a few times until successful.

Top tip

It is common for children to cheat a little (e.g. squinting when they should have their eyes closed). Don't worry too much, as they will keep their eyes closed as they gain in confidence.

Lost sheep 58

"This activity works well with plenty of space and is great fun."

This activity follows on well from the previous idea (see Idea 57). Children (the lost sheep) find their partner by sound alone, thus developing careful listening. They use vocal sounds, which have been shared first with their paired partners.

Age: 6–11

Resources: Plenty of clutter-free space; other adults (if possible)

It is a good idea to have other adults keeping an eye on the children during this activity, to avoid them venturing in completely the wrong direction, or bumping into each other on purpose.

● Children buddy-up (you or another adult making up a pair if there is an odd number of children; alternatively have a spare child as a helper).

● Children choose their individual vocal sound (farmyard sounds work well, but any fairly loud sounds will do).

● Each pair share their vocal sounds, so that they are very familiar with each other's sound.

● Children spread out around the area – and away from their partner.

● Explain to the children they are going to find their partners with their eyes closed, so they need to be cautious and sensible.

● When all eyes are closed, they make their sounds and find their partners (e.g. holding their arms when they find each other).

● Don't worry if a few children 'cheat' – especially if it makes them feel safer.

● Once they find their partner they stand in pairs and watch other children still seeking each other.

Top tip

If space is limited, or if it is expected the children might get over-excited, use half the children to make a safe circle in which the other pairs play the game, and then swap over.

Taking it further...

Play this game a few times, perhaps exploring new sounds, or sounds to given themes such as zoo animals, sounds of the seaside, modes of transport, etc.

59 Lighthouses

"This is great for developing social skills ... everyone was involved."

This activity follows on well from Idea 57. One child (the ship) is guided to another child (the safe harbour) by the vocal sounds made by the other members of the class who are the lighthouses (or sound houses in this instance). The 'ship' listens carefully to the sounds to be guided to the harbour.

Age: 6–11

Resources: Plenty of clutter-free space

All children choose their own vocal sound to use in this activity (see Idea 57).

○ Decide who will be the 'ship' and who will be the 'safe harbour'.

○ Everyone else finds their own space, allowing enough room for anyone to walk around them. (Children can find this quite difficult, so take time to organise them. Remind them it is like 'finding a space' in PE.)

○ The children (lighthouses) all face in one direction and stand straight and tall, making as narrow an obstacle for the ship as possible.

○ The 'ship' faces them (with eyes closed), whilst the 'safe harbour' child finds a place far away from the ship.

○ The 'safe harbour' child makes their sound constantly to guide the ship to them.

○ The 'lighthouses' make their vocal sound only when the ship moves near them, always turning on the spot to face the ship as it makes its passage to the harbour. Remind them that a good lighthouse will never allow a ship to come too close, or walk into them.

Top tip

If space is limited, or if it is expected the children might get over-excited, use half the children to make a safe circle in which the others play the game, and then swap over.

○ The child who is the 'ship' (eyes still closed) sets off to the safe harbour, directed by the sounds. You should stay close to the 'ship' for health and safety purposes.

○ When the ship reaches the harbour, the 'safe harbour' child places their hands on the shoulders of the 'ship' to let them know they have arrived safely.

○ Children are unlikely to mind if this activity is repeated a few times.

Hunt the mobile 60

"I'll remember this next time I lose my phone!"

Develop children's attention and listening skills with this simple seeking activity.

Age: 3–5

Resources: Two mobile phones, yours and another adult's (alternatively a small hand-held record/playback device such as Easi-Speak); xylophone (optional)

In advance of the lesson, set your mobile phone settings so that it will ring for at least 15 seconds.

● Select a child to be 'it'. They don't get to see where you hide your phone.

● Hide your phone and let all the other children see where it is hidden.

● The other adult rings your phone, and the child who is 'it' must find it before the ringing stops.

● Repeat the activity to allow different children to try and find the phone.

Developing the idea for older children

Older children can try finding a hidden object, directed by other children. You might sing a well-known class song, getting louder as the child nears the hidden object and quieter as they move away.

Taking it further...

Hide an object behind the back of a child sitting in a circle of children. The child who is 'it' walks around just inside the circle and attempts to stop at the child who has the hidden object. The seeking child is guided by you or a child playing higher notes on a xylophone as they get nearer, and lower notes as they move away.

61 Are your ears switched on?

"This really helped me understand form in music."

Children learn about the structure of the melody in a well-known song. They are encouraged to notice the use of repetition.

Age: 6–11

Resources: A set of three cards marked 'A' and one 'B' card; tuned percussion notes C D F G A; recording of *Old MacDonald had a farm* (optional)

❍ Sing or listen to a recording of *Old MacDonald had a farm* a few times.

❍ Children consider the melodies for the different phrases of the song. Are any of the melodies the same?

A	*Old Macdonald had a farm, E-i-e-i-o.*
A	*(And) on that farm he had a cow, E-i-e-i-o.*
B	*With a moo, moo here and a moo, moo there,* *Here a moo, there a moo, everywhere a moo, moo.*
A	*Old MacDonald had a farm, E-i-e-i-o.*

❍ The children should spot that the words and melody of the first and last phrases are the same.

❍ Do they also notice the second phrase has the same melody ('And on that farm'…)? (Strictly speaking, it has an additional note at the start of the melody to go with the word, 'And'. For the purpose of this activity this might be acknowledged, but the phrase is similar enough.)

❍ Notice that the third phrase is different. Use the 'A' and 'B' cards to show the structure of the melody (A–A–B–A) as shown above.

Invite confident individuals to try to play the complete melody by ear on tuned percussion.

A: F F F C   D D C   A A G G F

B: CC F F F CC F F F   FF F FF F FF FF F F

Taking it further...

Repeat this activity with the *Skye boat song*. The structure of its melody is A–A–B–B–A–A (you will need an additional 'B' card). It uses the notes C D F G A C'.

Bonus idea !

Leave a xylophone or set of chime bars (notes C D F G A) and the structure cards in the music area for children to try to work out how to play the melody of *Old MacDonald had a farm* themselves during the following week.

Noisy families 62

"The children had great fun creating their individual sounds and then composing a piece."

Children explore vocal sounds, and in the process the texture, timbre, dynamics and pitch of their voices. Once cards have been distributed you can either tell children the families to listen for, or ask them to decide for themselves once they hear the sounds.

Age: 4–7

Resources: Sets of picture cards for families of sounds (e.g. farmyard animals; modes of transport; onomatopoeia words like 'achoo'; machine sounds, etc.) – enough for everyone to have a card

You will need a large, clutter-free space to play this game.

● Distribute the sound cards randomly to the children. Explain that they must not show their card to anyone!

● Explain that the idea of the game, 'Noisy families', is to find others from your family by making your own sound and identifying other family sounds.

● Children find a space in the room and on a given signal they begin to make their sound. They circulate listening for other family members.

● The sounds should result in small groups of children gathering together.

● Ask children to sit down in their 'families'. Listen to each group making their sounds.

● Discuss whether everyone is in the right family.

Taking it further...

Children put their sounds together to make a short soundscape composition about their noisy family.

Bonus idea

Older children could create a graphic score of their piece with a key to explain their symbols (see Idea 48). Children could then read and interpret each other's graphic scores.

63 Visualise the music

"This really helped me understand structures and different timbres in music better."

Sometimes visual images can help to understand structure, timbre and pitch more easily. This idea is designed to help children understand the compositions of others by using visual prompts. It can be translated for use with any relatively simple piece.

Age: 9–11

Resources: Recording of *Dawn*, the first of Benjamin Britten's *Sea Interludes*; interactive whiteboard or pens and flipchart

Ask the children to listen quietly as you play them the recording of *Dawn*. Ask them what images came into their minds while they were listening – any answers will be 'right'.

Play the piece again, pausing at intervals to help the children notice different aspects in the music. Whilst listening, you (or a confident child) makes a drawing to represent what is heard, using a different colour for each sound:

○ First the high violin sound with a high single line slowly descending.

○ Ask children to listen out for a second very different sound (a sort of bubbly sound on clarinets) and then a third quiet rumble and hiss of deep drum and cymbal (represent these with a dotted line towards the bottom of your diagram).

○ Finally, help children identify the sound of trombones and other brass instruments that make up the fourth sound in this piece.

Top tip

Benjamin Britten wrote his *Sea Interludes* in 1945. The piece *Dawn* is about four minutes long and was one of four musical interludes from an opera called *Peter Grimes*. Each interlude depicts a different character or mood of the sea.

● Your diagram might look something like this:

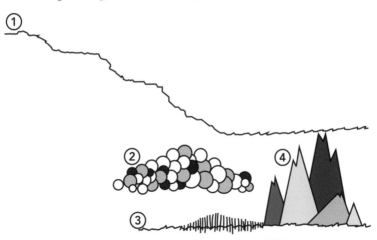

Listen to the recording again and follow your visual representation of the sequence of the four sounds. Discuss how the composer slightly altered the order and loudness of the four elements to make particular effects.

Taking it further...

Play Storm, Britten's fourth *Sea Interlude* from the Peter Grimes opera. Ask children to respond to the storm music visually by drawing or painting shapes and patterns suggested by the music.

Bonus idea !

Children could work in groups of five or six to create four musical ideas and arrange them into a piece in a similar way.

64 Card sort

"I had never realised how many different ways there were to describe what a piece is, and isn't."

Musical vocabulary is developed through debate whilst listening to music.

Age: 7–11

Resources: Sets of description and non-description cards (enough for each group); extract of recorded music (1–2 minutes duration); hoops

Before the lesson, research an extract of music and create a set of five or more 'description cards' (focusing on voices, instruments, time and place it originated, composer, tempo, mood, purpose for which it was written, etc.). This information can often be gleaned from a CD cover or an online source, etc.

For example, if you were to choose the opening of Beethoven's fifth symphony, you might include words such as: orchestra, powerful, quite fast, Beethoven, Europe.

Create five or more 'non-description cards' that don't describe the piece you have chosen, e.g. pop group, gentle, quite slow, Africa. Don't worry too much if you feel some words are ambiguous, as hopefully this will stimulate some discussion.

Organise the class in groups of around seven or eight, with each group sitting around a hoop. Share out a set of description and a set of non-descriptions cards to each group.

Taking it further...

Have some blank cards on which children can write their own describing words (both correct and incorrect) to use in the activity and add to the collection.

○ All listen to the extract of music and ask each group to place the cards inside the hoop if they feel the card describes the music, and outside the hoop if they don't.

○ If they feel very certain about a card they place it closer to the centre of the hoop.

○ After listening to the music and sorting the cards they compare results and discuss the music.

"The children had an amazing discussion, going far beyond anything I'd have expected."

Children work in groups to debate which piece of music is the 'odd one out'. The value of this activity is in the discussion and argument rather than getting a 'right' answer. Children develop their listening skills, and a technical language.

Age: 9–11

Resources: Three extracts of music (approx. 1–1½ minutes each)

This activity can be played on many occasions to introduce a variety of genres, periods, and styles of music. The aim of the game is for the children to pick the odd one out. You could have this in mind when choosing your listening pieces (e.g. two with keyboard and one without; two jazz pieces and one folk, etc.); however, you could just select three extracts for no particular reason – and see what the children decide (but note the Top tip). Keep your own reasons a secret from the children.

Divide the class into groups of seven or eight.

- Play the extracts and ask the groups to discuss what they can hear and what each piece may or may not have in common. Don't worry if the children talk about the music whilst they listen.

- After the children have heard all three they have to suggest which extract they think is the odd one, and why.

- Encourage as many reasons as possible. If they struggle for appropriate language, support them or encourage them to best describe their reasons.

- Introduce new words/phrases to support the children's music language.

- When groups have given reasons, reveal your own thoughts on which you felt was the odd one out. Children love it if you say you've changed your mind as a result of their arguments.

Top tip

This activity can be played on many occasions – but be aware if you tell the children there isn't an odd one out (if there isn't), it will spoil the activity for future occasions.

Taking it further...

Ask children, or groups of children, to create their own set of three listening extracts for the game to challenge the rest of the class.

66 Listening inspiration

"The children couldn't believe how magical their compositions sounded."

Here, the children listen to a piece of music and use the ideas to inspire their own creations.

Age: 7–11

Resources: recording (or YouTube clip) of *Cantus in Memoriam Benjamin Britten* by Arvo Pärt; as many sets of the notes A B C D E F G A' as possible (chime bars, xylophones, metallophones, keyboards)

Listening

Explain to the class that they are going to listen to a piece of music that was composed to remember a great musician who died in 1976 (Benjamin Britten).

Listen to the recording. Draw from the children their observations on:

○ the effects of the bell at the beginning and end

○ their ideas on the mood of the piece

○ the slow speed

○ the repetition of the falling step movements

○ the long sustained notes in the background.

Play the notes A' G F E D C B A slowly on tuned percussion or a keyboard (choose a bell sound). Start on the high A and go down step by step. Notice how these are the notes of the piece they have listened to.

Explain that these notes form a minor scale (A minor) which is why they might sound sad.

Divide the class into groups of six with as many tuned instruments as possible – ideally each group should have at least one complete set of notes for the scale (A B C D E F G A') with as many other individual notes from the scale as possible.

Top tip

You could quietly play the A minor scale whilst the recording is playing to help children notice how it has been used.

Composing

Encourage each group to create their own piece inspired by *Cantus in Memoriam Benjamin Britten* (approximately one minute of music). Encourage them to improvise to generate ideas using what musicians call a *minor scale*. They could include:

● the minor scale moving slowly or quickly and evenly or unevenly, in rhythmic patterns or with silent gaps

● long sustained notes in the background at intervals or throughout

● a single somber bell to start and finish as in the recording.

After about ten minutes, ask groups to share their ideas with the class. Use peer (whole class) assessment on each composed piece to discuss what was good, what was clever, what was effective, and what could be improved.

Return to groups to allow them time to polish their compositions for a final performance.

Taking it further...

You could repeat the composing activity using the C major scale (C D E F G A B C') and ask the children to describe any differences they notice in the feelings or images it evokes.

Bonus idea !

Listen to another piece of music by Arvo Pärt (e.g. *Spiegel im Spiegel*). Discuss with children the scenes they imagine, or different feelings they have while they are listening. Avoid suggesting there is a 'right' answer but use the exercise to illustrate the many different ways of thinking and responding to music.

67 The music of the playground

"Music is just everywhere — you don't need instruments."

As well as promoting awareness of their environment, this playground activity promotes creative thinking, exploring and using 'found' sounds. Children will compose on a large 'canvas', resulting in an environmental composition.

Age: 6–9

Resources: A drumstick or piece of dowelling per child; other adults (if available)

This activity takes place on the playground. Give each child a drumstick or piece of dowelling.

◗ Set off walking in a long line; set a slowish footstep beat: 1, 2, 1, 2, 1, 2, 1, 2… Make sure the children are walking in time with you to the beat.

◗ When the beat is established, walk towards a (solid) fence/wall. Stop and march on the spot. Then tap a rhythm pattern with your drum stick or dowel on the fence for the children to copy, e.g.

	1	2	1	2
You:	Tap	tap tap tap	rest	rest
Children:	Tap	tap tap tap	rest	rest
You:	Tap	rest	tap tap tap	rest
Children:	Tap	rest	tap tap tap	rest

◗ Continue walking 1, 2, 1, 2 towards some gravel/tarmac/dry leaves and make a new pattern, e.g.

	1	2	1	2
You:	Jump	scuf-fle	jump	scuf-fle
Children:	Jump	scuf-fle	jump	scuf-fle

● Divide the class into groups of around six and allocate each group to a sound-making place in the playground.

● Each group invents rhythms using whatever soundmakers they can find.

● Give them ten minutes to find sounds, invent patterns and then put them together to create a piece with the following criteria:

▸ The piece should be approximately one minute long.

▸ It should include six different rhythms.

▸ It should include a period of silence.

▸ It should have the structure ABA (first section; second section; first section repeated – see Idea 49)

● Each group performs their piece.

● Help children to choose words to make contrasting rhythms against a strong beat 1, 2, 1, 2, 1, 2, e.g.

Taking it further...

Perform the groups' pieces as a sequence, tapping the footprint ostinato to link each piece to the next, e.g. (footsteps) 1, 2, 1, 2, 1, 2, 1, 2 **PIECE 1** (footsteps) 1, 2, 1, 2, 1, 2, 1, 2 **PIECE 2** etc.

1	2	1	2
Tree:	Tree	tree	tree
flo-wers	flo-wers	flo-wers	flo-wers
pit-ta pat-ta:	pit-ta pat-ta:	pit-ta pat-ta:	pit-ta pat-ta:
rub-bish bin	rub-bish bin	rub-bish bin	rub-bish bin

68 Sounds around us

"I never realised there were so many sounds all around."

Top tip

Model the activity to the children before asking them to do the task themselves.

Taking it further...

Ask children to give detailed descriptions of sounds, for example instead of writing 'birds', or 'birds singing', they might write, 'high squeaking bird sound' or 'harsh chattering metallic bird sound'. These could then be used to make more complex sounds (timbres) to use in the bonus idea below.

Bonus idea

Back in the classroom, use classroom instruments to recreate the minute of sound heard on the playground. The children move with their instruments to recreate the orientation and movement of sounds they heard.

Children are naturally inquisitive about their environment. This activity builds on their enjoyment of outdoor spaces, promoting sound discrimination and description and orientation of environmental sounds.

Age: 7–11

Resources: 'Spatialisation' sheets (see below); pencils and a clipboard

This activity should take place outdoors.

○ Children, in pairs, scatter themselves around different areas.

○ They stay completely silent and listen to the sounds they hear around them for one minute.

○ They record the sounds they hear in words or pictures on their spatialisation sheet as they listen and afterwards in discussion with their partners. They should indicate:

▸ which direction sounds are coming from

▸ how far away the sounds are

▸ how loud or soft they are

▸ what quality the sounds have (e.g. metallic, wooden, rubbing, rustling, etc.)

▸ whether the sound is moving from one place to another.

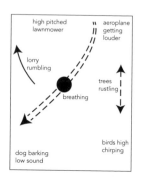

Open doors

"We listened really carefully to the differences in the sound of cars and lorries."

Children listen for sounds beyond the classroom – predominantly focusing on dynamics and timbre. They explore percussion and other soundmakers to recreate the sounds in their own compositions.

Age: 7–11

Resources: Prepared laminated photos/cards of the most likely sound sources

This activity is to be done inside, but somewhere with a door to open to the outside.

● Ask children to be silent and listen for sounds outside.

● After 30 seconds open the door to the outside for a minute. Ask children to call out things they can hear (lorries, cars, aeroplanes, lawnmowers, birds, building site sounds, people talking/playing, etc.).

● Repeat the process after hearing answers.

● When five or six different sounds have been identified, ask volunteers to try to represent/recreate the sounds on classroom/other instruments or voices.

● Volunteers demonstrate 'door open' volume and 'door closed' volume with their sounds.

● Divide the class into groups, each group representing one of the sounds.

● Groups practise loud and soft versions of their sound.

● Appoint a conductor who uses the photo cards of lorries etc. to indicate which group should 'play', inventing hand signs to indicate whether sounds should be loud (door open) or soft (door closed).

Top tip

Teach the Italian words 'piano' (quiet) and 'forte' (loud). Ask the conductor to use these words to control the volume (dynamics) of the sounds with their hand gestures.

Taking it further...

The conductor now directs groups to gradually get louder or quieter (the Italian words are 'crescendo' and 'diminuendo') to represent the gradual opening or closing of a door. The groups layer their sounds to make a structured composition, e.g.

Birds   Birds   Birds   Birds   Bird
[silence ---] LORRY LORRY lorry lorry lorry
car car [silence ---] car car car car car car

Bonus idea

Make a structure with different patterns using start and stop, forte and piano, crescendo and decrescendo.

70 Making a sound map

"I love it when we go out of class!"

By taking a group on a short walk around a busy area, children can focus on sounds in the human environment near their school. Translating real-world sounds into musical approximations deepens children's understanding of timbre and pitch.

Age: 8–11

Resources: Three simple maps of 100-metre sections of streets near the school (each map should have about five places A – E marked clearly on it, with room for written annotations); large-scale version of the combined maps; audio recorders or mobile phones (optional)

This is a good activity to link with other subjects like geography and history, where every locality can become a unique and valuable resource.

○ Divide the class into three groups (10–12 children in each group).

○ Take each group on a different short walk following one of the three prepared maps. Choose streets with contrasting characters.

○ As you pass the places marked on the map (e.g. a coffee shop, a butchers shop, a garden, construction site and office), ask children to note down or record sounds they can hear that tell something about the activities going on there.

Taking it further...

Make an interactive wall display map of the different journeys, with press-buttons linked to recordings of the different sounds children reproduced. Perform the sound map to the rest of the school.

○ Draw attention to details like different pitches of bird song, what instrument the scraping of chairs sounds like, how to describe the clink of cups, buzz of machinery, hum of electricity or drone of passing traffic ... and don't forget the silences.

○ Back in class, groups use instruments to reproduce the characteristic sounds of each stopping place A – E.

○ A 'conductor' uses a large-scale version of the map to direct players. The conductor decides the direction of travel and tempo of the journey.

Bonus idea

Children make a sound map of their own choice of journey.

○ Invent a 'linking theme' to represent walking between the places on the map.

Musical school trip

"I really liked trying to imitate the sound of the leopard — it sounded like a rumble."

This activity takes place during a class visit to a zoo/wildlife park. It has a cross-curricular approach, developing skills and knowledge in science and art. The children listen carefully to animal sounds to develop their aural discrimination, and then reproduce the sounds back in the classroom.

Age: 8–11

Resources: Laminated photographs of different animal markings (elephant, tiger, zebra, fox, wolf, owl, depending on the animals encountered on your visit) for each group; drawing paper, pencils and clipboards; a selection of percussion instruments and other sound sources

Before they set off, give each group one of the laminated photographs of an animal's markings. During their visit, each group needs to identify their animal from the markings and then spend 15–20 minutes getting to know it:

● The children carefully draw 'their' animal.

● Whilst drawing, ask children to listen for sounds that the animal makes or causes, e.g. breathing, panting, padding, splashing, grunting, roaring, etc.

● Children add 'sound' descriptions around their drawing.

● If there is no noise, the movement of the animal or sounds or words of people watching might be noted.

Back at school, children use their notes and video recordings of the species, to reproduce the sounds or represent the animal's movements with their voices or instruments.

The animal skin photographs can be arranged on a wall and used as prompts, or a musical score for a conductor as they direct groups to play their animal sounds music in turn.

Top tip

This activity can be adapted for use with other class visits.

Taking it further...

Make an interactive wall display map of children's drawings (and perhaps additional artwork based on them) with a looped recording of the composed animal sounds activated by the button beneath.

Bonus idea

Children could make sound pictures of different world habitats by representing the sounds of the animals of the jungle, desert, savannah, Antarctic, etc.

72 Expressing emotions in music

"Taking photos for our music is great."

Children collect photos depicting a range of emotions, then create short musical ideas to match the emotions shown, thinking about how pitch, dynamics, timbre, dynamics, tempo (speed), rhythm and duration (length of sound) can express mood.

Age: 5–7

Resources: Make a set of 'emotional frames' – A4-sized sugar paper viewfinders, with words for basic emotions written on (e.g. happy, sad, scared, calm, peaceful, angry, interested, etc.); cameras for the children to use; a selection of tuned and untuned percussion and other soundmakers

○ Divide the class into groups of five or six children.

○ Allocate one emotional frame to each group.

○ Take each group individually on a walk around the room or playground. They look for faces, views or things, etc. that somehow match the emotion word written on their frame.

○ When they have found something they feel matches the emotion, children take its photo through the frame, deliberately including the part of the frame with the 'emotion word' in the picture (so that they know later what the theme was).

○ Give each child an opportunity to choose and take a photograph.

Top tip

Discuss ideas with children, e.g. what makes a sound feel sad? What tempo might scary music be? What rhythms would sound happy? What dynamics might we associate with peacefulness? (See also Idea 50.)

● When each child has taken a photo, return to the classroom to explore soundmakers that might match the emotion on the framed photos.

● Invite volunteers to create sounds to match each mood. Discuss which sounds seem most appropriate (e.g. upward-moving high and quick movements on a metallic instrument for 'happy').

● Set each group the task of making their improvised emotion sounds more prolonged and refined.

Taking it further...

Children create a longer composition (e.g. lasting one minute) that includes contrasting emotions, e.g. happy – sad – happy (see also Idea 49).

Bonus idea

Ask children to make up secret mood music to play to the rest of the class and get the rest of the class to guess what mood or moods they are trying to evoke.

sad

happy

angry

73 Building patterns

"How can you play those battlements in sound?"

This activity focuses on structure and timbre in musical composition. It uses buildings as a kind of musical score that children can use to compose well-balanced, satisfying and original pieces.

Top tip

Find photos of more complex buildings for more advanced groups to translate into music. The challenge of how to represent an arch or battlements or an onion dome in musical sound will provoke very creative results. See Idea 49, for help using the capital letters for musical structures.

Bonus idea

String musical buildings together into a street or town of musically-represented structures. Children could add finesse by varying dynamics according to depth of colour or changing the timbre according to materials used in the building.

Age: 6–9

Resources: Collect photos of buildings (houses, castles, cathedrals, mosques, temples, etc.) or organise a time outside the classroom where children can view a number of buildings; a selection of tuned and untuned percussion

Demonstrate this activity first as a class, then ask children to compose in small groups.

● Choose one photograph – perhaps of a simple bungalow – and show children how it can be made into the structure of a composition, e.g. wall – window – door – window – wall: A B C B A.

● Ask the whole class to use found sounds around them to invent a short musical idea that reminds them of a brick wall (section A). Then ask for another sonic impression of a glass window (B) and another to evoke a solid wooden door (C).

● String these three sounds together and then reverse them to make a simple composition based on the bungalow facade.

● Distribute photographs of different buildings and ask groups to represent them in sound in similar ways, using appropriate timbres and textures to denote the building materials (stone, wood, brick, slate, glass, tiles, etc.).

Journey sticks

"This is a fantastic non–musical starting point for music–making!"

Children often need a structure to help them shape their music. This exercise gets children outside the classroom and uses non-musical starting points to help them create their own original music.

Age: 7–11

Resources: Journey sticks (enough for one between two) – strips of card or real sticks with double-sided tape stuck to one side; a selection of classroom instruments

Take groups of children for a short walk in the playground, forest school or other outside location. Give pairs of children a journey stick.

Each pair must agree, pick up and stick six small found objects (no living things!) to their journey stick and remember where they found it.

Demonstrate how the journey stick can become a musical score for an improvised piece. Explain that the pairs will need to choose appropriate sounds for each of their six objects (using classroom instruments, 'found' sounds, body percussion or vocal sounds) and improvise musical ideas for each, e.g.

1. Gravel – might suggest a rapid shaker sound

2. Earth – a smooth continuous sound with the sand blocks

3. Forget-me-not flower – makes a happy jingly sound with three chime bars

4. Leaf – makes a much smoother and more shapely sound with a metal beater scratched on a cymbal

5. Smaller leaf – makes a smaller sound than before because the leaf is smaller

6. Forget-me-not – repeats 3.

Pairs of children make up music from their journey stick in a similar way.

Taking it further...

Ask children to lengthen their pieces to one minute and then perform their journey stick to the rest of the class. You could also join the results with a simple joining melody invented by a class violinist/recorder player/guitarist.

Bonus idea

Display images of the journey maps and journey sticks on a PowerPoint presentation with a musical backing composed by the children.

75 Blowing up an equatorial rainstorm

"This has worked really with every year group in Key Stage 2."

Becoming involved in a directed whole class musical composition can really stimulate and exercise children's imagination. This activity is teacher-directed, but the control of sounds and ideas can quickly be passed to children.

Age: 7–11

Resources: None

Children need to be sitting in a fairly tight circle with no breaks. Explain that the activity is designed to help them appreciate what a rainstorm sounds like in the equatorial rainforest.

Explain that you are going to pass sounds around the circle in an anti-clockwise direction. Each child should ONLY listen to and watch for the sound made by the child on their left.

○ Start in absolute quiet.

○ Begin to make the first sound – the rubbing of dry hands together.

○ When the child on your right hears and understands the sound, they start making the sound too, then the child to their right joins the sound, then the next, and so on.

○ Once the first sound has made its way halfway around the circle, change your sound to an irregular sharp tap of two fingers on the palm of the hand. The child on your right changes their sound accordingly, and so on. (Note that some children will still be starting the first sound as the second sound starts being passed around.)

Top tip

The challenge in this activity is for children to wait until the child on their left gives them each sound, and not simply copy what their teacher does. Choose a confident and well-focused child to sit on your left and remind children frequently to watch and listen to the child on their left.

● Gradually make the tapping sounds more regular and increase the tempo. Imagine the rain getting heavier.

● One by one introduce new sounds in the same way, always waiting for the previous sound to have made its way halfway round the circle before introducing the next sound. Make the sounds build in intensity, e.g. clap quick beats, slap hands on thighs, strike the floor as loudly as possible in front of you with open hands.

● When you have reached the most intense sounds (e.g. everyone is beating their hands on the floor), reduce the intensity by going back down the order of sounds until you are rubbing hands together and finally silence.

● When children are more confident with this activity, make it more dramatic by building in intensity and reducing intensity several times before reducing back down to silence.

Afterwards, discuss the activity. Ask the children question, such as:

● What did they imagine happening in the piece?

● What did they think the sound on the floor might represent?

● What might the rubbing of palms at the beginning and end of the sequence represent?

● How might a British rainstorm be different to the equatorial rainstorm they have just created?

Taking it further...

Watch the videoclip 'Human thunderstorm' at **dwheway. wikispaces. com/100+ideas+ Music** Encourage confident children to have a go at leading the activity.

Bonus idea

Listen to some pieces of music which describe a storm, e.g. Beethoven's 6th Symphony fourth movement; *Summer* from Vivaldi's *Four seasons*; Richard Strauss' *Alpine Symphony (Thunder and Storm, Descent)*; Britten's *Storm* from *Four sea interludes*; Whitacre's *Cloudburst*. Comparing these pieces could be part of an extended listening activity on a single theme (see What's my line? – Idea 56).

76 Finding patterns in the environment

"There are just loads of patterns everywhere."

There are patterns all around us and this idea explores how rhythm and structure suggested by patterns can help children invent new musical ideas.

Age: 5–8

Resources: A checklist sheet with illustrations of common local patterns for children to spot (for each child) or paper for children to draw their own; pencils and clipboards; a selection of tuned and untuned percussion

Top tip

Help individuals and groups refine their offerings by stressing regularity of pulse and consistency of sound.

Taking it further...

Make a musically-illustrated backing track to a series of excellently-framed photographs taken on the class iPad to share with other classes.

Bonus idea

Combine the musical ideas children invent for shapes like rectangles and circles and patterns like those in brickwork, to build a musical house!

● On a walk, children spot features like the long-short-long-short pattern of brickwork, steps, zigzags, spots, grids, curves, circles, arches, squares and triangles, etc.

● They record what they see by completing a pre-prepared checklist or by drawing.

● Back in class, experiment with musical responses to their shapes and patterns, asking questions such as, 'What could the repeated pattern of dots on our carpet sound like?', 'How could we make a sound that suggests a circle?'

● Children work in small groups to explore and develop their ideas.

● Use the sounds as backing for a sequence of photographic images that inspired them.

Pattern	Where did you find it?
	√ School door √
	School wall
	drain cover
	kitchen floor √

Getting started with
music technology

"I am not sure what hardware and software I will need."

This idea offers some practical hints and tips for ideas suggested in this section.

○ iPads/tablets and PCs – activities in this section suggest one iPad/tablet/computer between pairs or groups, but demonstrating from an IWB (Interactive Whiteboard) (see connectors below) with a whole class can also be very effective.

○ VGA, Lightning or HDMI connectors – connect from the device to the screen or IWB. Apple products will require a specific connector. Ask your IT friend/colleague which you need!

○ Remote connections – instead of using connectors, you may be able to connect using Bluetooth, Apple TV or other apps. Your IT friend/colleague should be able to advise.

○ Speakers – children's work sounds much better if connected to some external speakers or the IWB, rather than listening through the device's in-built speakers.

○ Headphones – these can be really useful when children are working on their own ideas in pairs or groups. Note that attaching headphones to a device can sometimes mute the volume – so check.

○ Splitters and leads, with mini-jacks – splitters connect multiple sets of headphones to the same device (so more than one child can listen through headphones). Splitters come with two or more sockets. They can often be bought cheaply from large supermarkets.

Top tip

Headphones can be harmful if the volume is too high. Encourage children to move the volume control down then ease it up to a comfortable level. As a general rule, if you can hear sounds from their headphones – they are probably set at too high a volume.

Taking it further...

The apps and programs suggested in the following activities are all correct at time of publication. However, technology is continually being updated and developed, so the following link provides further supporting information and regular updates: **dwheway.wikispaces. com/100+ideas+ Music**

78 Pictures in sound

"I love the combination of children's instant art and sound."

In this simple activity children draw sounds as they are made, then play the drawings. The result is instantaneous, and very gratifying. How the picture is played is open to the inventiveness of the child.

Age: 3–5 (particularly good for children with SEND)

Resources: iPads with the app **Singing Fingers** (ideally one iPad for two children to share)

Following an introduction from you, children explore the app **Singing Fingers** following the procedure given below:

● **Open the app** by clicking on the **Singing Fingers** picture. The app opens to a drawing board (with some framed help pictures and video guides to the top right of the screen).

● **Make sounds vocally** at the same time as you draw a picture with your finger(s). The app records the sounds whilst you draw on the screen.

● **Play the picture** by sliding your finger across, or by tapping at different points in the picture. Try moving through the picture in different ways (backwards, finger skipping, slide and a tap, etc.).

● **Save the sound picture** when the child is happy with the picture and the sounds by pressing the 'floppy disk' blue icon at the top left of the drawing pad.

● **Start a new picture** by tapping the blank page icon top left of the screen.

● **Find a previous picture** by tapping the 'open folder' icon top left of the screen.

Top tip

It is always worth becoming familiar with an app before using it with your class. Help on apps/programs used in this resource can be found at **dwheway.wikispaces. com/100+ideas+ Music**

Taking it further...

Working in pairs, one child records, whilst their partner creates sounds on percussion, found sounds, sounds around the classroom, animal sounds, etc.

"This is a really effective way to compose music!"

Many apps inspire children to play rhythm machines. They can use iPads as beatboxes or drum kits (e.g. MyDrumsetFree, VidRhythm, John Cage Piano, My BeatBox). This idea uses MadPad HD. It allows children to record their own sounds to the rhythm grid. The result is a beatbox, and/or an additional percussion instrument.

Age: 8–11

Resources: iPads (enough for one between four children); **MadPad HD**

It would be beneficial if children have first done some work with 'Rhythm grids' and 'Exploring vocal sounds' (see Ideas 20 and 57).

● Allow children to explore the app for a few minutes.

● Next, on the home screen, click on 'Create your own sets'.

● On the next screen, for the moment select 'Try this'.

● If there are any pictures in the cells, just click on 'Clear all'.

● As a child looks at the screen, they'll see a moving image of themselves.

● They tap 'record' on any cell and simultaneously make a short vocal sound.

● The cell stops recording after approximately five seconds, or when the input sound stops. Short sounds might be best initially.

● Once each child has recorded a sound, they should tap the cells in a sequence to create interesting rhythms (and see a brief video of themselves).

● Once all 12 cells are filled, they can tap on 'Save and play'. Enter a 'Title' and 'Creator' name.

● Children continue exploring the rhythm grid they have made, or go to 'Home' and 'Browse sets' to explore their own or others' sets.

Top tip

Become familiar using this app before using it with your class. **dwheway.wikispaces. com/100+ideas+ Music**

Taking it further...

Children experiment playing with the pads to create interesting rhythmic sequences. They practise maintaining a steady rhythm, and could possibly team up with others to create rhythmic ensembles.

80 Music Mike Create

"I enjoyed creating our piece and playing it to the rest of the class."

Creative music technology doesn't need to be complex. Music Mike Create is easily understood by the youngest child, whilst being an excellent starting point for anyone wishing to understand how to undertake very simple editing.

Age: All (particularly good for children with SEND)

Resources: iPads (enough for one between four children or one linked to the interactive whiteboard); **Music Mike Create** (for iPad)

Exploring vocal sounds

Use the activity 'Exploring vocal sounds' (Idea 57) as a way for the children to generate their own short vocal sounds to use in this activity.

Demonstrate the activity working as a whole class at first, then divide the class into groups of four to create their own compositions.

Recording and altering their sounds

Home screen

● Each child in the group records their sound into one for the four different coloured pads (red, yellow, green or blue).

● To record, they select the record icon (red circle with a white dot in the centre). When fully red, they tap their chosen coloured pad. The pad will fill with colour as the recording is made (up to five seconds).

● They might need a couple of goes to make a good recording. The clearer the recording the better for this activity.

Editing screen

● Once all children are happy with the recording of their sound, they tap the icon.

○ They then tap any coloured pad to make the sound play as a loop.

○ Encourage them to explore tapping on the different character pictures to alter the sound (e.g. to change the volume, pitch or speed or to play the sound backwards).

○ When they are satisfied with their changes, they scroll down the screen to find and press the magic wand icon to save.

Mixing a final piece

Mixing/recording screen

○ Once the group has saved changes to all four of their sounds, they tap and hold the record icon to go to the mixing screen.

○ They explore potential mixes by pressing and holding all edited pads – singly and in combination, thus exploring texture and structure.

○ When ready, children make a recording (perhaps limit this to 15–25 seconds). The record icon starts a timer, and is also used to stop the recording.

○ Children will be prompted to give the mix a name. Mixes are saved to the home screen, where they can be played (and shared).

Taking it further...

Invite each group to perform their final mixes to the class. If possible, play them through the interactive whiteboard or external speakers, rather than the device speakers, as the sound is so much better which boosts the children's confidence and self-esteem.

81 Sound collage

"Some of their sound collages sounded truly unique."

Children record their own sounds and explore ways to structure and combine them using sequencing software, to compose a sound collage.

Age: 7–11

Resources: Computers with sequencing software **Audacity** or iPads/tablets with sequencing apps **Audacity**, **Music Mike Create** or **MixPad** (enough for small groups to share or one connected to the interactive whiteboard for a whole class activity); USB microphone if using a PC/laptop

The sound collage might simply be a collage of random sounds edited for effect, or could relate to a real or imagined event, e.g. to provide a backdrop for creative writing, drama, an assembly, a school production, etc.

● The children decide which sounds they would like to record.

● They record them using **Audacity** (see opposite) or similar software/apps.

● They choose three or four sounds to use in their composition and explore ways in the software to alter the sound and to combine the sounds to create different structures and textures for their sound collage.

● Once they have decided on a sound collage they like, they mix their file down.

Play your piece/s to another class or upload them to the school's website or an electronic display board in the school reception area.

The instructions given opposite are for using **Audacity** on the computer. However, the activity can be completed using apps (such as the ones listed above). These instructions are correct at time of publication, however **Audacity** is updated regularly, so may need adapting slightly for your version.

Taking it further...

Challenge the children to listen carefully to their final mix, and attempt to recreate their sound collage with percussion, voices, instruments and 'found' sounds. This may be impossible as the sequencer can produce really quite unique sounds, but the process will involve the children thinking and exploring, and will result in a new composition.

● A USB microphone is currently a good option for recording sounds and can be bought quite cheaply. It slots into a USB port in your PC or laptop. iPads have an internal microphone which is fine.

● Press the red record button (top left of screen); you will see the recording being made.

● Try a sample recording to ensure everything is working correctly.

● Go to 'File' drop-down menu, and click on 'Export Audio'.

● Note where the file is saved (or create a destination folder).

● Record and export other short sounds.

● Go to the file drop-down menu and select 'Import' then 'Audio'. Note that you can import other saved sound files on your computer as well as any you have recorded.

● Use 'Ctrl' and click to select three or four sounds to import (note that sounds must be 'imported' rather than 'opened').

● Under the drop-down menu 'View', select either 'Fit vertically' or 'Fit in window'.

● Move files around using the shift icon at the top of the screen («), and dragging files to left or right.

● The class, or group, agrees on an arrangement they like.

● Explore ways to change sounds further using the 'Effects' menu.

● Once happy, export your file (go to: File – Export Audio) which will mix it down into a single mono or stereo track.

Top tip

Try the program/app first before using it with your class. There is help on using **Audacity, Music Mike Create** and many other apps at **dwheway. wikispaces.com/100 +ideas+Music**

82 Contrasting environments

"This is a great idea for linking with other schools."

The children record sounds from their local environment and combine them using sequencing software to create a sound collage of their local environment. This can be shared with a school in another place, linking nicely with geography.

Resources: Computers with sequencing software **Audacity** or iPads/tablets with sequencing apps **Audacity**, **Music Mike Create** or **MixPad** (enough for small groups to share or one connected to the interactive whiteboard for a whole class activity); USB microphone if using a PC/laptop

This activity can build on ideas from the 'Music in the environment' section of this book, such as 'Sounds around us' (Idea 68) or 'Making a sound map' (Idea 70).

At some point you will need to agree with your linked school (which might be nationally or internationally), to sharing sound collages of your different locations.

● The children should make a collection of sounds from their local environment. These might be short, 'on location' audio recordings, or sounds they have recreated using a variety of sound sources (vocal, body, found, percussion, instrumental).

● Follow the instructions on using your own recordings to make a sound collage using **Audacity** in the previous idea (see Idea 81) – or adapt them for using a mixing app such as **Music Mike Create** or **MixPad**.

● Edit the recording until you are happy that it is an accurate representation of your location, either literally or in feeling/emotion.

● Export the mix, so that it is saved as a single track (exporting the mix will do this automatically).

● Exchange your mix with your linked school.

Top tip

Try to get as close as possible to the sound source so that it is to the fore of the recording.

Taking it further...

Groups of children could create mixes from different places within their local environment.

"Mixing loops is really cool!"

Children practise layering repeating rhythms then develop them using sequencing software.

Age: 9–11

Resources: Selection of untuned percussion; iPads/tablets/PCs (one between two–four children or one connected to the interactive whiteboard); sequencer software, e.g. **Soundtrap** PC/android/iOS (free online using Chrome); alternatives are: **GarageBand**, **Loopseque**, **Loopy HD** or **MixPad** (iPad); **ReLoop** or **PocketBand** (Android)

Suggestion: start with recalling the activity 'Riff my rhythm' (see Idea 42)

Divide the class into groups to create a piece. The instructions below are for the app **Soundtrap**, which is free online using 'Google Chrome'.

● Each group explores the loops in the soundbanks in the software. Loops can be found at the top right of the screen in a purple circle with music notes. They should play automatically as they are selected.

● When they have found loops they want to use, they drag their choices across left and align under '1' in the tracks window. They add further loops. **Soundtrap** automatically adds and plays each loop.

● Loops can be started and stopped using the standard play/stop icons at the bottom of the screen.

● Children can alter the volume of each track by finding the volume wheel in the left-hand controls.

● Loop mixes can be saved (see 'Save' at the top of the screen above the tracks). The song can be given a name by clicking on 'Untitled Song', also above the tracks.

> **Top tip**
>
> The terms 'ostinato', 'riff' and 'loop' all essentially mean the same thing but in different contexts: 'ostinato' is the generic term for a repeating pattern; 'riff' is a repeating pattern particularly in pop music and jazz; 'loop' is a repeating pattern using technology.

> **Bonus idea**
>
> Successful compositions can also be exported (under File) as mp3s for sharing.

84 The strong one!

"Now I understand about the 'strong beat', I feel more confident to lead rhythm games."

This simple activity helps children to experience the beat aurally and visually and to gain better understanding of the strong beat in music.

Age: 7–11

Resources: One PC/Mac connected to the interactive whiteboard; **Hydrogen** freeware for PC/Mac (alternatives: **orDrumbox** (freeware for PC/Mac); **Loopseque** or **Loopseque Lite** for iPad); a selection of tapping percussion (claves, woodblocks, drums, tambours, agogos, etc.)

This is a whole class activity.

Set up the strong beat

○ **Open Hydrogen:** this brings up a window with ten blank patterns to fill (patterns are numbered 1–10). The beat numbers go along the top; the instruments are listed in rows (tracks) down the left side. (If other windows open, e.g. 'Mixer' and/or 'Instrument', they can be closed for this activity').

○ **Set a steady beat** by selecting the 'Tempo' window (which might be difficult to see; it is at the top of the screen.) The tempo will be set to 120 by default, which is quite fast, so slow it down to 80 by double-clicking on the number 120 and typing 80 (or use the down arrow keys until you get to 80).

○ **Select Pattern 1** in the upper grid – if it isn't already selected.

○ **Choose instruments to play on beat 1:** Choose a few instruments to play on beat 1 by clicking the instrument's track under the number '1'.

Top tip

When you count the beat in music, the strong beat is count 'one'. Being able to feel the strong beat in music is important for keeping time.

Pattern 1	1	2	3	4
Kick	●			
Stick	●			

o Select the play icon – at the top of the page (again this can be tricky to spot initially, but it is a standard play icon triangle). The tracks you selected will now play on beat 1 in a loop. Ask children to clap the strong beat with the program.

Add rhythm patterns

o Create rhythm patterns: Invite a volunteer to select another instrument, and create an interesting rhythm pattern by clicking anywhere along the track. Try not to fill the tracks too much or the rhythms can sound 'crowded'.

o Can children clap this rhythm? If it is difficult, adapt the rhythm (ensure dots are not too close together), or slow down the tempo.

o Create more rhythms.

o Perform the track: Divide the class into groups, one group playing/clapping/stomping on the strong beat, whilst other groups play along to one or more rhythm tracks from the grid.

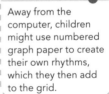

Taking it further...

In the top grid – select Pattern 2 to create a new set of tracks. When playing back it is possible to click on Pattern 1 then Pattern 2 and so on to switch between patterns.

Bonus idea

Away from the computer, children might use numbered graph paper to create their own rhythms, which they then add to the grid.

85 Rhythm words rip

"Children enjoyed trying to keep in time with themselves."

Children create and record word rhythms using a sampling app.

Age: 8–11

Resources: iPads/tablets (one between four children or one connected to the interactive whiteboard for a whole class activity); **Keezy** app (iPad) or **BeatBox** app (Android)

Children invent simple word sequences (perhaps connected to a topic) and practise performing them to a steady beat (see also Idea 42):

○ Count in 1 2 3 4, then say/clap the word rhythm to a steady beat.

1	2	3	4
Anne	Tu-dor	Kath-er-ine	Parr

Divide the class into groups of four to create and practise their own spoken/clapped sequences.

The groups record their sequences using a sampling app (e.g. **Keezy** or **BeatBox**). The instructions below are for **Keezy**.

○ **Open the app and make a recording:** Press the black circle. Press the + symbol. Recording begins as soon as you tap the microphone symbol. Tap again to stop and store.

○ **Play back two or more pads to check recordings are in time:** It may take several attempts to get their word sequences to play back in time with each other.

○ **Re-record on any pads:** Press the black circle, tap the red X. A black cross will appear on the pad/s. Tap to reinstate the microphone. Record again.

○ **Save their 'board':** Press the black circle, then the lines for 'file'. Tap the open circle on 'untitled'. Type in a name then ✓.

Children explore structure by tapping on single, or combinations of, pads in a sequence.

○ Touch the black circle. Choose the 'reel-to-reel' (jam session) icon to record. Play one or more pads together.

○ Tap the reel-to-reel icon to play back the recording.

○ Recordings can be saved to various places. Tap the arrow at the bottom of the screen.

Gone all loopy

"I get it now, the rhythm changes but fits with the beat."

Children explore creating and combining loops.

Age: 9–11

Resources: iPads (enough for one between pairs or small groups); iPad app **Loopseque** (or **Loopseque lite**)

● Introduce the app and explain that each of the four circular grids represents a different sound: red – drum; yellow – bass; purple – percussion; green – lead instrument.

● Demonstrate first how to create loops to pairs/small groups. You/The children experiment clicking on different cells to explore rhythm patterns.

Using Loopseque

These instructions are for the full version, but they can be adapted for the 'lite' version.

● **To open the app** – tap the screen, select 'New Project' then 'Create'.

● **To add a drum pattern** – tap the red grid. Activate the drum by tapping cells to create rhythm patterns. Symmetrical patterns often work well.

● **To stop/start the sound** – tap the white bar below the circles x (stop) or o (start).

● **To change the tempo** – select the top right 'cog' symbol.

● **To add another instrument** – tap the yellow/purple/green circle. Activate the segments as before.

● **To adjust the volume** – slide the control up or down.

Top tip

As you open the app you can choose 'Master Class'. This is a very useful introduction to using **Loopseque**. Go to **dwheway.wikispaces.com/100+ideas+Music** for further support and updates for this activity.

Taking it further...

Children can record their completed loop, save it and give it a name. It can then be reloaded to use another time or be sent via email.

Bonus idea

The multiple grids layout allows children to explore rhythmic patterns more, by enabling them to switch between different patterns.

87 Strum a chord

"It's so easy to play using a guitar app."

With no guitar skills, anyone can provide guitar accompaniment using a virtual guitar.

Age: 9–11

Resources: Song lyrics on whiteboard; iPads/Macs with **GarageBand**; alternatives: **Baby Chords** (iPad) or **Walk Band** (Android)

The song below only uses two chords: C major (C) and D minor (Dm).

◉ Open **GarageBand**. Go to 'Smart Guitar'. (You might need to press 'back' if the app has been used recently.)

◉ Change the 'key' by clicking on the spanner icon, then 'Key'.

◉ Select 'D', then 'minor'. Tap the main screen to return to the guitar.

◉ Tap the chord names just above the strings (or strum the strings).

◉ Play the sequence of chords shown below.

Dm	Dm	Dm	Dm

What shall we do with a   drun - ken   sai - lor?

C	C	C	C

What shall we do with a   drun - ken   sai - lor?

Dm	Dm	Dm	Dm

What shall we do with a   drun - ken   sai - lor?

C	C	Dm	Dm

Ear   ly   in   the   mor   -   ning.

◉ Try different styles using the dial 'AUTOPLAY'.

◉ Rehearse singing *Drunken sailor* without accompaniment to remind the children of the song.

◉ Sing the song again with guitar accompaniment, e.g.:

▸ A group of children play the accompaniment on a number of iPads.

▸ The teacher/one confident child plays the accompaniment.

▸ Allocate each chord to a different group of children (useful if children struggle to switch between chords). Help by pointing to each group when they should play.

"We made an 'app' pop group!"

Children form an iPad ensemble to use as an accompaniment to the song *Drunken sailor*. They utilise the skills developed in Ideas 86 and 87 to accompany the song.

Age: 10–11

Resources: iPads/tablets with **Loopseque** (or **Loopseque Lite**) and **GarageBand**; children's own instruments, such as ukuleles or guitars (optional)

This activity might offer a circus of activities, where children develop skills on iPads and singing as well as their own instruments. Organise half the class to sing, and half to provide accompaniment. Swap groups to ensure all children develop skills in singing and teachnology.

○ Chord accompaniment group: Learn to play the chord accompaniment to *Drunken sailor* using **Garageband** (see Idea 87) adding any instruments children can play, if available (such as guitar/ukulele). Rehearse strumming the strings in the software.

○ Rhythm group: Create percussion and bass accompaniment in **Loopseque** or **Loopseque Lite** (see Idea 86), using all but the green circle. Set the beats per minute (bpm) to 80 using the top cog icon (this can be speeded up/slowed down later as required). It's best only to use one iPad for the rhythm group as it can be challenging to sync rhythms across multiple iPads!

Combine everyone on iPads and instruments as well as singers to perform *Drunken sailor*. Decide how many beats of the accompaniment to count in before the singers enter.

Top tip

Go to **dwheway. wikispaces.com/100 +ideas+Music** for further support and updates for this activity.

Bonus idea

These songs also use just two chords: *Three is a magic number* (Jack Johnson): E and A; *Eleanor Rigby* (The Beatles): Dm and C *A Ram Sam Sam, Pizza Hut* song: D and G; *Kookaburra*, D and G (or even just D); *I am the music man, London bridge, Pease pudding hot, O my darlin' Clementine* (all traditional): F and C

89 Baby chords

"The app really helps to find the notes for the chords."

Children use technology to learn about chords. They create the chords of C major (C) and G major (G) to accompany a song, and transfer the chords onto different instruments.

Age: 10–11

Resources: iPads/tablets (enough for one between four children initially to explore, and then to form a small accompanying group when singing); **Baby Chords** app; selection of tuned percussion; ukuleles or guitars if children play them

The **Baby Chords** app is a fantastic introduction to chords, and children at the top of KS2 love it!

❍ Explain to the class that a chord is two or more notes played together.

❍ Use the app **Baby chords** to create some simple chords: tap the notes C, E and G together (this might need two children tapping together). A balloon will float upwards labelled with the name of the chord 'C major'.

❍ Now children find the same notes on tuned percussion. Suggest they play the notes as a block chord (all at the same time), with two beaters in one hand and one in the other, or play with a partner.

❍ Using the app **Baby chords**, tap the notes G, B and D together – this is the chord of G major.

❍ Find the same notes on tuned percussion, as before.

Top tip

Go to **dwheway. wikispaces.com/100 +ideas+Music** for further support and updates for this activity.

● Play the chordal accompaniment to *The Pizza Hut song* (which is to the same tune as *A Ram Sam Sam*, so either song might be used) using apps and tuned percussion. Invite children who can play the guitar or ukulele to play as well. Sing along.

	C		**C**		**C**		**C**
A	*ram*	*sam*	*sam,*	*a*	*ram*	*sam*	*sam*

	G		**G**			**C**		**C**
Gu - li	*gu - li*	*gu - li*	*gu - li*	*gu - li*		*ram*	*sam*	*sam.*

	C		**C**		**C**		**C**
A	*ram*	*sam*	*sam,*	*a*	*ram*	*sam*	*sam*

	G		**G**			**C**		**C**
Gu - li	*gu - li*	*gu - li*	*gu - li*	*gu - li*		*ram*	*sam*	*sam.*

	C		**C**		**C**		**C**
A	*ra*	*-*	*fi,*	*a*	*ra*	*-*	*fi*

	G		**G**			**C**		**C**
Gu - li	*gu - li*	*gu - li*	*gu - li*	*gu - li*		*ram*	*sam*	*sam.*

	C		**C**		**C**		**C**
A	*ra*	*-*	*fi,*	*a*	*ra*	*-*	*fi*

	G		**G**			**C**		**C**
Gu - li	*gu - li*	*gu - li*	*gu - li*	*gu - li*		*ram*	*sam*	*sam.*

Taking it further...

Find more chords on the **Baby Chords** app. Divide into three groups – each group sings a different note of the chord. Explore singing the three notes of the chord separately and then together (in harmony).

90 Backing track

"My children find this activity so much fun!"

Children will enjoy creating a pop/jazz style backing track.

Age: 10–11

Resources: iPads (or Macs) with **GarageBand** software (ideally one each or one between two); headphones and splitters

These instructions are for **GarageBand** (correct at time of publication).

● **Open GarageBand**. Go to 'My Songs' (top left of screen.)

● **Create a new song** – click on the + symbol then 'Create New Song'.

● **Add a drum rhythm**. Scroll left or right through the instrument sets until you find 'Drummer'. Select 'Acoustic Drums'. Press the play button. The cursor moves from the left through each bar playing a drum riff.

● ▫▫ **Add guitar chords** – click on the top left symbol next to 'My Songs'.

● Within 'Guitar', select 'Smart Guitar'.

● Notice eight chords lying across the strings. Explore strumming the strings or touching the top of the chord bars for a chord to play automatically.

● Try moving between the chords C, F and G major only. If these aren't obviously available, select the spanner icon (top left), then: 'Edit Chords'.

– Tap the far left chord. Above the strings you'll now find scroll wheels.

– Scroll the far left scroll wheel to select 'C', and in the second scroll wheel from the left select 'Maj'.

– Now for the second and third chords from the left, select 'F' and 'Maj' and 'G' and 'Maj' respectively.

– Press 'done'.

● **Set the tempo**. Select the spanner icon and set 'Tempo' to 90.

● **Return to the main screen** by tapping the side of the guitar.

C / / / C / / / F / / / G / / / C / / / C / / / G / / / C / / /

● **Press the play icon** to play the following sequence (strum the chords or use one of the 'autoplay' settings):

● Try changing the F chord to F minor using the scroll wheel. Does the mood of the sequence feel different?

"How do I discuss music with children when I feel my own knowledge is limited?"

It is perfectly fine to discover music with the children, rather than expect to be the expert. Finding out about different composers, genres of music, instruments, etc. will help develop children's opinions about music.

Age: 10–11

Resources: Internet access; headphones and headphone splitters (so groups of children can share a computer/iPad/tablet, each with their own set of headphones)

What to prepare

● Should children learn something specific, or enjoy exploring and finding out for themselves? Restricting their search within a specific website can help ensure similar aspects are learned. A guidance sheet can also be helpful.

● Does the site include audio tracks in preference to lots of facts?

● Perhaps have some broad ideas you wish children to explore (e.g. instruments around the world, the music of Poland…).

● Rather than browse the whole site, encourage children to listen to an extract a few times.

● Finding sites to explore might appear daunting. There are a few current suggested sites below. The website 'Listening links and topics' at **dwheway.wikispaces. com/100+ideas+Music** is regularly maintained with up-to-date links.

> **Top tip**
>
> Beforehand, check access to website/s with your technician. Ensure safeguarding is well-embedded and children know exactly what they can and cannot do whilst on the Internet.

Useful questions

- Can you find some music you would like to share with others?

- Can you identify/does the website tell you which instruments are playing?

- Can you identify any specific musical 'elements' within the music (pitch, dynamics, rhythm, structure, tempo, texture, timbre)?

- Was the music written for a specific occasion, purpose?

Useful websites

Some sites may require players such as Shockwave, so check with your IT technician.

- **mydsco.com/dso-kids**

- **nyphilkids.org**

- **realworldrecords.com**

"I can't teach music — I'm not musical!"

These points below address some of the most common concerns that primary class teachers have about teaching music.

I can't read music

'Stave' notation isn't used in this book. Many musicians around the world don't use stave notations. We have, however, suggested other ways of notating sound.

I'm tone deaf

This is highly unlikely – but you are possibly anxious of using your singing voice.

Children are rarely critical of a teacher's voice – they'll appreciate the opportunities you provide. If your spoken voice is able to rise and fall in pitch – so can your singing voice.

I don't know what to teach

The emphasis in music should be regular practice, to develop: beat and rhythm, musical elements (see Idea 28), playing, using voices, creating music, performing own/others' music, critical listening to own/others' music.

I don't know how to assess music

Here are simple observations you can make:

- Do children listen with attention?

- Do they sing clearly?

- Do they follow the brief?

- Do they build on other children's ideas?

- Do they speed up a rhythm or keep a regular pulse?

Top tip

Be prepared to have a go – children will respect you for it. Let them know if you are trying out an idea for the first time, and if you struggle (for instance in a rhythm game), let the children take the lead.

● Do they go beyond the brief and produce something with originality?

I don't know how to gain attention when all children are playing

Introduce a signal. Children enjoy looking for small signs (e.g. you standing in a certain position in the room, holding a beater quietly in the air). Be prepared to wait. Remember, if they are slow to respond, perhaps they are engrossed in the task you have set!

I don't know what listening music to play to the children

Listening critically is more important than selecting the 'right' sort of music.

Start by listening to music familiar to you. You will feel more confident discussing it with children. In time, develop your listening to incorporate music from a range of genres (styles), traditions and from different parts of the world.

Staff in other classrooms complain about the noise

Diplomatically point out that you are meeting the statutory requirement to provide music to your class (as are they…surely?). However, do warn other teachers if you expect a session to be especially noisy. Take the opportunity to explain what the children have been learning.

I don't have enough different ideas

Building a stock of music activity resources is vitally important. However, an excellent way to learn new activities is by talking to colleagues in your own and neighbouring schools and seeking advice from people steeped in primary music approaches which are inclusive (see Ideas 93–95).

Bonus idea !

Ask the children to stand whenever possible for music activities – it helps them begin to feel the beat through their bodies and maintain a better posture for singing. And bear in mind how much children already have to sit within a school day.

"Where do I go for further music support?"

Music is unusual in having few teachers, even within local families of schools, who feel qualified to advise. However, there is support that can be tapped into.

Make links with local schools

Meeting up with other teachers is a good way to share ideas and resources. Bringing schools together is also a good way of buying in advice, perhaps for a CPD day or twilight music workshop.

Local music hub

Make contact with your local music hub, as they can help in many ways (see Idea 94).

Publishers

Publishers often have someone, including authors, who they can call on to meet your needs and provide training.

Music conferences

These are organised both locally and nationally. Check your local hub website and the websites mentioned below. Or, attend local events to get to hear of other opportunities.

National organisations

These can also be very supportive – and put on regular CPD, e.g.

● Orff Society UK (**orff.org.uk**) – this is probably the closest in approach to the ideas in this book. They often organise training in your locality, and would be very pleased to hear from you.

Taking it further...

Is there a nearby HEI (Higher Education Institute) that may have someone on their teaching staff who could support you? The local authority/other schools may know of an expert in your locality who works in a freelance capacity.

- Dalcroze UK (**dalcroze.org.uk**)

- The *British Kodály* Academy (**britishkodalyacademy.org**)

CME – Certificate for Music Educators (Level 4)

This national qualification is validated by Trinity College London. It is for anyone teaching music in schools (not just qualified teachers). Your hub may well be part of the training, or may know of a local CME centre. Information on the CME and current centres is available at **http://www.trinitycollege.co.uk**

ISM (The Incorporated Society of Musicians) – **ism.org**

This organisation is fast developing its support for schools and teachers working at all levels.

Music Mark – musicmark.org.uk

Music Mark tends to represent music services/hubs – but it is keen to develop support for teachers in schools and may be able to help you locate local support.

"Is a music hub the same as the old music service?"

Music hubs are organisations responsible for overseeing music education, instrumental teaching, local community facilities and practitioners and for bringing musicians together to develop excellent practice in your locality.

If your school receives instrumental teaching from your local hub, your teacher with a responsibility for music may be in regular dialogue with the instrumentalist or local music hub. If not, make contact – they usually have a website.

● Find out what they have by way of CPD.

● Find out what they offer for whole class teaching of instruments.

● They may also offer projects working with professional musicians – find out about any funding that may be available.

● Check for the annual conference – this is a great way to network with like-minded teachers.

● Your hub may well run Saturday or evening music centres. Encourage your children to join these, especially your gifted and talented.

● They may also offer summer schools or holiday music courses. These can be great fun and a lovely way to develop your musicians.

● Hubs may organise local music festivals or events for your choir or instrumentalists. Sometimes they are able to offer teaching support to prepare your musicians for the day. You can learn much from watching project leaders.

Top tip

Liaising with local hubs should be to your mutual benefit. The local hub can bring a high level of music expertise to a liaison with a school, whilst a school can bring high levels ofunderstanding of pedagogy, including inclusive practice, SEND, EAL, behaviour for learning, professional practice, etc.

95 Secondary links

"It is important to build links with the receiving secondary school music department."

This idea discusses ways to build links with your receiving secondary schools. It is particularly relevant for teachers in Years 5 and 6 and those with responsibility for music.

Meet up with your receiving secondary music teacher/s

○ Tell them what you are doing in class music and about other musical activities in school. They may be unaware of such activities.

○ Don't be daunted by their musical expertise (as they shouldn't be daunted by your broad pedagogical knowledge and expertise).

○ Ask how they intend to build on the experiences your children have had whether through classroom music or instrumental lessons.

○ Consider a joint event, perhaps showcasing work from both schools.

○ Mention any Gifted and Talented pupils, giving details of their experience and qualifications if appropriate.

What support can they offer?

○ Does your secondary colleague know something about primary music? They may be happy to share ideas.

○ Do they have students who might share their work with your pupils?

○ Are there resources they might lend your school, such as a drum kit, electric guitar, West African drums, etc.?

○ Can you visit and use their facilities?

> ### Top tip
>
> Your secondary colleagues are also busy people with deadlines, exams and performance targets. Ask them to suggest a suitable point in the year to meet and discuss children. Take examples of work.

Local music teacher's support group

Some secondary schools have 50 or more feeder primary schools. Is there a local music group where information can be shared?

Transition

Some schools plan transition projects for Year 6 children going into Year 7. This is a great way for teachers to share knowledge about children. The children can find out about music activities and clubs on offer, too.

Working with instrumental teachers

"The children love sharing pieces they are learning."

Many schools have visiting instrumental teachers. Get to know them. As well as making them feel welcome in your school, it can open up avenues of support.

○ Some instrumental teachers are willing to lead extra-curricular music groups. This might require additional budgeting but a working partnership such as this can prove invaluable.

○ They may be willing to perform their instrument on their own or in a group in an assembly or concert – this can often lead to a greater take-up of their instrument, so is mutually beneficial.

○ They can support children learning an instrument to build on ideas in your classroom music project, e.g. to learn the melody for song, practise improvisation ideas, etc.

○ If they are linked to a local music hub, they might also be able to share initiatives designed for primary teachers, such as courses and resources.

Once you have built up a good working relationship with them, you may find you can turn to them for curriculum music support, e.g: to interpret resource materials; to help teachers to understand musical activities and concepts; to offer advice for developing class music lessons which is not over-specialised.

Consider, also, how you might value the instrumentalist's contributions to your children's broader education:

○ Does your school allow time for instrumentalists to set up their work space and reflect on your pupils' learning?

○ Does the school demonstrate how such lessons are valued by having the class teacher attending large group/class instrumental lessons and working alongside the instrumentalist?

○ Does the school share a common vision of music development with visiting instrumentalists?

Top tip

If possible, ensure they have one person they can communicate with on a regular basis, and keep them informed about changes to the school diary that might impact on their teaching time.

97 Percussion storage

"It takes me an age to collect percussion for lessons!"

Thinking carefully about how percussion is stored can help maintenance and save time setting up.

Consider having a set of instruments in each classroom, so that music can occur during the week, and children can choose music in free time (e.g. in 'Golden Time'). Wherever you keep your instruments, you need to consider how to store them so they are easy to access and use in your lessons.

Music trolleys: these are quite costly, and have many disadvantages, especially if you need to move music across playgrounds, up or down stairs, over rough surfaces, etc. Items can get damaged in baskets when children pull them out, so check the viability of a trolley before purchase.

Storage boxes and buckets: these work really well. Having an assortment of about 10–15 items in each large box means you only need to collect two or three boxes for a music session. A bucket or two to keep all beaters in means they won't get easily lost, and can be handed out last and collected in first.

Some schools store all similar items in boxes (e.g. a box of triangles, a box of maracas…). This can be troublesome, as each time instruments are required it is you who has to make up a collection.

Larger instruments

Tuned percussion (xylophones, metallophones, glockenspiels, chime bars) and other large instruments (e.g. keyboards), are often difficult to store and to transport to the classroom. Larger items should be carried by two people. It is important to include larger instruments in your activities to add depth to children's playing. Consider having some items in each classroom, so they be can be borrowed from nearby and not carried too far.

Top tip

Have instrument 'monitors' – children who have the responsibility of checking and caring for the percussion. Children love the responsibility! You could give some older children the job of collecting and setting up the boxes in a classroom.

"This is a really handy guide!"

This idea offers guidance on building and maintaining your collection of classroom percussion.

There are basically three categories of untuned percussion: tappers, shakers and scrapers. The lists below detail some fairly common instruments. An assortment is preferable to too many of the same instrument. Consider instruments from different countries, too.

Tappers are instruments that are tapped with the hand(s) or beaters: drums, djembes, tambours, bongos, frame drums, claves, woodblocks, two-tone blocks, agogos, lollipop drum, triangles, cymbals, slit tongue or gato drums, boomwhackers, finger cymbals and Indian or temple bells, tulip blocks and temple blocks.

Wear and tear: Drums, bongos and tambours may have replaceable skins for when they break. Reduce wear and tear by playing with hands unless a beater is essential. Many instruments will need disposing of when they break, for health and safety reasons.

Shakers include tambourines, maracas, stick castanets, chocolas, bells, nutshell shakers.

Wear and tear: The skin on tambourines gets torn. Maracas split after time or lose their handles, bells fall off bell shakers, and nutshells fall off nutshell shakers. Most of these will eventually not be worth keeping. Expect to replace fairly regularly.

Scrapers include cabasas, guiros, click-clacks.

Wear and tear: Beads round cabasas can work loose in time – but for a while can be secured by re-tightening the handle. Guiros split in time, and the guiro scrapers tend to go missing – but just use a beater handle. Click clacks can work loose over time.

Sound effects are instruments that might be used occasionally for effect, and include rainmaker, ocean drum, spring drum, vibra-slap, spring drum and flexitone.

Top tip

Avoid storing any of the above in wire storage crates as it reduces their life further. They tend to get trapped in the wires then break/ weaken when pulled out.

99 Percussion care and maintenance – tuned

"We have some tuned percussion but it's beginning to look old."

Tuned percussion is expensive, but if cared for can last for years.

Tuned percussion includes: xylophones (wooden or resin bars), metallophones (thick-ish metal bars), glockenspiels (thin metal bars), chime bars or hand chimes (single pitches). Xylophones and metallophones are usually sold in three sizes (bass, alto, soprano). Glockenspiels tend to be soprano and alto.

Sets usually include beaters and the notes C D E F G A B C D E F G A with some extra F sharps and B flats. Some schools also buy all the sharps and flats (equivalent to the black notes on a keyboard).

Care and maintenance

Sound chambers on xylophones and metallophones for some reason become filled with old crayons, straws, broken beaters and an excessive amount of dust. A regular clean-out shows this is valued equipment.

Anecdote 💬

Many years ago (well, about 25), an author of a book of music ideas was asked for advice on purchasing new xylophones for a school. They had a budget of £800. He slashed and hacked and repaired them all, because he liked that school. The total cost was £20. 'Hurrah', exclaimed the headteacher, but still went on to spend the £800, making it one of the best-stocked schools in the area, and everyone lived happily ever after.

Over time, the rubber mounts on which bars sit start to break or perish. Repairs with Blu-tack™ don't work. The reason is because the Blu-Tack™ won't allow the bars to vibrate. A repair kit from a percussion stockist is only a few pounds, and will make the instrument almost as good as new.

Pins on which the rubber mounts sit can bend, meaning bars can't vibrate or may even rest against neighbouring bars. Demonstrate to children how to remove bars without bending the pins: one hand at each end of the bar and lift straight up. DO NOT lift one end only! If pins are fairly thin, they can be straightened by hand, but a pair of pliers is better.

Chime bars (especially the tubular variety) tend to work loose on their stands over time. Some carefully-applied glue can work as a mend, but eventually they'll need replacing.

"Performances are real highlights in the school calendar!"

Ensure children have lots of opportunity to perform within and beyond your classroom music lessons. Performances can range from the short and informal to larger 'showcase' settings.

Celebrating children's work

Organise mini-performances to showcase your children's achievements in classroom music lessons (e.g. clapping a two-part rhythm to a high standard, singing with clear diction, representing a mood word in a small group – where each member of the group is aware of when to start and stop their sound). Such performances might only take a minute or so:

○ Perform to other children in your class, or to another class.

○ Perform in assembly.

○ Perform to the children's preferred audience – their parents/carers. Consider a brief performance at the end of a school day – before the children return home with their parents/carers. (Consider alerting parent/carers to arrive slightly earlier so the school day still ends on time.

Assemblies

Small and informal performances in assemblies can increase the awareness of staff and other children of progress in music-making. This also helps to raise the profile of music and the self-esteem of the children.

Larger-scale performances

These require advance planning. Other members of staff and parents can really help. Here are some things to consider:

○ Venue (e.g. local secondary school hall or town theatre) – booking, risk assessments, health and safety, transport for children and/or instruments, backstage supervision, lighting and sound plans, timing.

Top tip

If your setting opts for a whole school performance it should involve all children and staff and is a great (if a bit stressful) way to contribute to social cohesion. It's also something the children will remember forever!

- What to perform – whole school or year groups or classes? For an end of term performance, a 5 minute class composition/performance from each class ensures the concert isn't too long (90 minutes or 2 hours with an interval is plenty long enough), and all children get to perform.

- What to wear – is there a need for costumes or uniforms?

- Supervision of children.

- Advertising – costs, programmes, master of ceremonies.

- Backing tracks or live band – can the local secondary provide musicians? Is there a parent, someone connected to the school who can accompany. Consider organising a parent-staff band.

- Rehearsal schedule – lunchtimes and after-school times – availability of children and teachers.

- Ticket sales/printing – liaise with the school office, or the box office if appropriate.

- Recordings – you will probably need permission from the copyright authority and also permission from parents for video recording.

- Creating a CD – what is the cost? How much can you sell them for?